Mary Hartwell Catherwood

The Queen of the Swamp

And other plain Americans

Mary Hartwell Catherwood

The Queen of the Swamp
And other plain Americans

ISBN/EAN: 9783337322809

Printed in Europe, USA, Canada, Australia, Japan

Cover: Foto ©Andreas Hilbeck / pixelio.de

More available books at **www.hansebooks.com**

THE QUEEN OF THE SWAMP

And Other Plain Americans

BY

MARY HARTWELL CATHERWOOD

BOSTON AND NEW YORK
HOUGHTON, MIFFLIN AND COMPANY
The Riverside Press, Cambridge
1900

TO THE MEMORY OF MY MOTHER

NOTE

SOME of these stories were written more than a dozen years ago. They have been gathered in from the Atlantic Monthly, Harper's Bazar, Outing, the Independent, the Delineator, the Chicago Tribune, the late Chicago Graphic, and Lippincott's Magazine, by courteous permission of the editors; and revised year after year. Many of them embody phases of American life which have entirely passed away, or are yet to be found in secluded spots like eddies along the margin of the nation's progress. Their honest preservation of middle western experience makes them, at least in the author's eyes, seem worthy themselves of preservation.

The Puritan and the Church of England took possession of the Atlantic seaboard, north and south; and Jesuit and Recollet missionaries carried the cross through Canada and down the Mississippi. But the pioneer evangelist of the Middle West was the Methodist itinerant.

CONTENTS

The Babe Jerome, Rose Day, The Bride of Arne Sandstrom, The Fairfield Poet, and *Beetrus* are reprinted from "Harper's Bazar," and *The Queen of the Swamp* from Harper's "Christmas," by permission of the publishers, Messrs Harper & Brothers.

OHIO

THE QUEEN OF THE SWAMP

On Christmas Day a large congregation
poured from George's Chapel into the early
dusk. Quarterly meeting, which for a week
had drawn together, not only the neighborhood, but people from Millersport, Basil,
and even Kirkersville, closed that afternoon.
The presiding elder and his assistants were
wrapping up their throats and joking with
each other, for the occasion had been blessed
with converts and a fairly liberal collection.

These men must ride on around the circuit, risking health, and accepting whatever
fell to their lot, yet nothing checked their
flow of spirits. The only solemn person
near the group was Mr. Warner, a local
preacher and exhorter, who habitually prayed
with a war-whoop, and kept the young people

tittering at his pompous phrases. His father, an aged apparition, tottering on a
stick, was circulating genially to shake
every hand, known or unknown, and inquire, toothlessly, "Hi-ya! hi-ya! how's
your consarn?" which being interpreted
meant, "How are you, how are you, how's
your concern?" (in religion).

Women clustered together near the red-
hot stove, exclaiming to each other, as their
work-worn palms met, "Hoddy-do, Mis'
Waddell, does your family keep well?"
and "Law! Mis' Davis, it's good for sore
eyes to see you out to meetin' once more!"
"Yes, I been kept close all fall, but I told
him it wouldn't do, we must come to big
meetin'." "It's been a good time. One
o' my boys," the speaker pressing her neighbor's hand, "was gathered in, and I have
my suspicions the other's touched." "Yes,
there's more under conviction than 'll own
to it."

They made excuses to each other for
neglecting neighborly duties in the past, but

promised, now such good sleighin' had set in, to go more. One had had whooping-cough in her family, another a teething baby, and not a few had been very busy getting the butchering done and making sausage. The men-folks were also constantly hauling with the teams.

Warm Christian feeling pervaded the whole separating assembly, even the young girls greeting each other with unusual affection. The young men drove their conveyances up to the door, exchanging merry remarks; there were many fine horses, and some of the sleighs were painted, but the general vehicle was a wagon-bed, stuffed with straw and comforters, and running on two short sleds called "bobs."

Theophilus Gill's sleigh was of this pattern, and he intended to drive the young folks to Macauley's. His spirited team pranced so that he stood up to control it, though at full height Theophilus Gill was but a little fellow. He had, however, a strong black beard.

"How many goin' in our load, Theoph?" inquired Philip Welchammer, resting one foot on the forward runner.

"'Bout ten couple. Mart, he's got to take his mother home, so he won't be along."

"You feel like as if you could spare him?"

"I always ken. Now, don't you go to cut me out if I try to engage her company for Sunday night."

"Oh, you and Mart fer it," said Philip. "I ain't fer cuttin' neither of ye out. But Persilla Thompson's a pretty girl."

"She's the Queen of the Swamp," said little Gill, with emphasis.

Priscilla at this moment stepped down from the chapel threshold into the snow, to wait for her party. Philip brought her to the sled and Gill insisted on placing her in a warm and sheltered place just behind the driver's bench, which he had specially prepared for her.

"Macauley's is makin' a big housewarmin' this Chris'mas," remarked Priscilla's little suitor to her. "They's four tables full of old folks to their turkey-roast, and the young folks all invited in the evenin'. I reckon the old lady's doin' it for Mart. She's bound for him to marry that Miller girl, some says."

Priscilla replied, with pleasant nonchalance, she reckoned so. She did not look at Mart Macauley at all, but she saw him watching her while he untied his bay filly, and held its head until his mother finished talking with her dinner guests.

He had loved Priscilla Thompson when she was a little girl with black plaits of hair hanging down her linsey back. In those days he gave her a bead purse, and whipped all her tormentors. When she began to be a big girl he shyly courted her, stopping his plough by the fence if he saw her coming, and dropping in of a Sunday night to see her brother, whom he despised, and who had since married and left him without excuse for his visits. When she got a certificate

and went into the Kemmerer neighborhood
to teach school, with her clothes neatly
packed in a large wicker basket, he had no
peace of mind all summer. He had himself
been to Worthington to college, but in all
his experience saw no one to compare with
her. Wherever he saw her, so modest and
lovely in manner, he cherished the ground
her shoes rested on. The cold air gave her
a bright color, which the depth and length
of her bonnet could not conceal. She wore
a wadded alpaca cloak and cloak cape, and
Martin's memory showed him how trimly
under these her delaine dress was coat-
sleeved to her arm and pointed at her
waist.

Mrs. Macauley, climbing into her own
sleigh, could take no exceptions to Priscilla
Thompson's manner or appearance, though
she would have done so gladly for the bene-
fit of her favorite son. Mrs. Macauley dis-
liked the Thompsons. Her husband before
his death objected to them. She thought
little Theophilus Gill the best match in the

neighborhood for Priscilla Thompson. Her own large light-haired son was too dutiful to marry without her consent. She was educating him to be a doctor; the younger boys could work the farm under her direction. She expected Martin to do his family credit by looking higher than the Thompsons.

Priscilla, on her part, held Mrs. Macauley in secret aversion. She felt sorry for Martin's younger brothers and sisters, who were all obliged to stand in a row and take pills or tincture before breakfast. Mrs. Macauley was too high-handed and all-prevailing. Priscilla's disposition was cheerful, but that Ohio region known as the Swamp could not escape the tinge of the period, and at that date the extremely feminine woman with a bias toward melancholy was the standard. Mrs. Macauley was so mannish that Priscilla thought her fully entitled to the tufts of beard in her moles.

The young people crowded merrily into Theophilus Gill's sled. They all knew how

matters stood between the Macauleys and
Thompsons. The Thompsons, excepting
Priscilla, who was a reticent girl, talked
about the Macauleys, and the Macauleys
held their heads rather high, excepting
Mart; but he thought the world of his
mother. The girls suspected Priscilla was
going to-night because her staying away
would make talk. Some of them believed
Theophilus Gill would get her, and others
thought things might take a turn so that
she would marry Mart Macauley after all.

There was a day when she would have
given half her life to go to Macauley's, but
stayed away. That was when Martin broke
his collar-bone racing his bay filly. Nobody knew that she hid in her father's
field corn-crib all that day. Yet it was not
an occasion for extravagant fears. Mrs.
Macauley was the best nurse in Fairfield
County, and soon had her son mended to
perfection.

A few flakes of snow fell on Gill's load,
and made it all the merrier. No joke could

fail to strike fire at once on the steel-clear air, and many a time-honored one was repeated by the young men as their fathers before them had repeated it, and enjoyed by the girls as their mothers had enjoyed it.

Philip Welchammer was pitied for having his arm out of place, and Nora Waddell, discovering it at that instant around her, told him tartly there *is* folks that their room's better than their comp'ny. Upon this he genially retorted that she never made no such fuss when they were out sleigh-ridin' alone; and Nora glowed in her red merino hood while the laugh turned upon her.

Then a girl's voice, to cover her confusion, started a thrilling old revival hymn, and the load poured its bass and treble through the lines. Darkness approached as near as the white world would allow. The triumphant strain echoed among treetops and stirred emotion in Priscilla.

" There, there on eagles' wings I soar,
And sense and sin are felt no more.

There heaven comes down our souls to greet,
And glory crowns the Mercy Seat —
And glo-ry crowns the Mer-cy Seat."

The road was bounded by that distinctively American fence, the rail, or stake-and-ridered, showing drifts of snow in its angles, and white lines like illuminations along the top of every lichened rail. The sled flew over corduroy spaces now deeply bedded. On each side the trees rose out of frozen pools, from which they seemed to conduct a glazed coating upward, for every twig glinted icily through the dusk. In springtime, when the Feeder and creek rose out of banks, acres of this swamp lay under water, with moss scum and rotting leaves at the top and bottom.

Priscilla found always in these woods a solemn beauty. Her wildest dream was of living deep in their summer shade with an unnamed person, and sitting on the doorstep at nightfall, her hand locked in his. The amber lights, the cry of tree-frog and locust, the mysterious snap of twigs, the reverberating bark of a dog, the ceaseless motion of water under a foot-log, all gave her delight. One spring she worked in her father's sugar-camp. A bark shelter that they passed reminded her of it, of collecting the sugar-water, watching the bubbling kettles, and dropping the wax on snow, of stirring off, which was such a festival, and at the same time such a miracle, for you could feel the hardening wax grain to sugar on your tongue.

Theophilus Gill turned his horses from the road, and drove through a gap into the woods.

" What are you doin' that for ? " exclaimed John Davis, who loved a horse, like every good Ohio man, but was always ready to sacrifice it to his comfort or speed.

Theophilus explained there was a bad bit of road ahead, and the circuit through the woods might be better.

If he dreaded cutting his team's ankles, the danger was not lessened by this choice of routes. For after some easy progress and much winding among saplings and jarring against stumps, they descended to a seldom-used bridge across the Feeder, standing like an island in a frozen lake. Theophilus Gill drew up his horses. There was not room in which to turn back, and the occupants of the sled rose with some apprehension.

Nora Waddell said she would never go over that bridge. Theophilus observed doubtfully he'd risk gettin' the team across, but mebby some of the boys had better walk over and lighten the load.

Everybody alighted except the driver, who cautiously, and reassuring his snorting horses, moved across the ice and up the bridge. It shook under their tread to such a degree that nearly all the party resolved to trust the ice in preference, and pushed their tracks carefully upon the snow-covered Feeder. Besides Nora Waddell, Philip Welchammer took under his charge Mary Thompson, Priscilla's flighty young sister, who was barely fifteen and in short dresses, but so headstrong that she would go into company whenever Priscilla did. Starts and exclamations were finally blended into a general outcry, for the ice gave way, and several figures disappeared to their very necks. Then the young men who had landed were prompt in action, while some of the girls showed courage and pioneer swiftness of resource. Philip and his two companions were pulled out, and huddled, dripping, into the sled, all available covering being piled upon them. Everybody scrambled in, and Theophilus, restraining his horses, asked, in an excited shout, if they were all in. Mary Thompson, through her chattering teeth, retorted, "Of course all of us were in, and if he did not mean to kill us entirely, he'd better whip up and get to some fireplace."

Thus reproached, and by the Swamp Queen's sister, the young man drove with such zeal that his horses ran away, and were restrained from tearing the vehicle

to bits against logs and fences only by his
utmost strength and horsemanship.

Thus the party came like a whirlwind
up the open lane to Macauley's, and were
hurried into the three-story house, while
Macauley's boys led the horses away to a
barn of similar magnitude, where long rows
of stalls and shining flanks were discernible
by lantern-light.

No less than three fireplaces had blazing
logs piled to the very chimney throats.
Sarah Macauley conducted the girls upstairs to the best room, from which opened
a bedchamber where they laid off their
wraps. The young men found a similar
haven on the other side of the staircase.
And it was pleasant to hear the logs snap
while frost lay so thick on the two upper
porches which were let into the sides of the
house.

Macauleys were very well off indeed.
The estate consisted of fifteen thousand
dollars cash, besides a couple of farms, and
the largest homestead in the township. Mr.

Macauley had accumulated all this, after breaking up twice during his career, paying security debts. Nearly all the floors were carpeted in home-made stripe or hit-or-miss, and the best beds reared backs as lofty and imposing as the backs of elephants.

Numbers of young women, arrived before this party, were basking in the best room, their hair and collars smoothed, and their eyes taking keen neighborly notes while the hum of conversation went on. Miss Miller from Millersport was there, and appeared a worthy rival for Priscilla Thompson. She had pink cheeks, and pretty brown hair on a low, delicate forehead, these charms being distractingly set in an all-wool blue merino dress and ribbon headdress to match. Miss Miller possessed two thousand dollars in her own right, and would come in for all her father's property when he died. Besides, she had attended select school in Lancaster, and some said she was so fine she would cut a bean in two rather than lift the whole of it on the point of her knife to her very pretty mouth.

Mrs. Macauley lost not an instant in dos-
ing her drenched guests with hot whiskey
and ginger stew. Other raiment was provided for them. When all the young people had arrived and warmed themselves,
they were to descend to the dining-room,
one of the largest apartments ever seen in
those days, supported by a row of posts
across the centre, and floored by oak as
smooth as glass. The name of kitchen
would have fitted it as well, for here the
family cooked. One of those new-fashioned
iron machines called stoves stood beside the
fireplace, having a pipe to carry its smoke
into the chimney. But Mrs. Macauley often
said it was not half as much use to her as
the Dutch ovens she always baked in, over
the coals.

A line of chairs waited around the sides
of the dining-room. The pantry, opening
at one end, half revealed stacks of Christmas provisions on shelves.

But there was to be no such godless
amusement as dancing. The young people

would frolic and play plays with kissing penalties, which could by no means corrupt them as much as joining hands and jumping to the tune of a fiddle.

Groups were already descending to the dining-room, and Mary Thompson struggled hard to hook one of Sarah Macauley's dresses over her stouter waist.

" Your sister did n't come?" remarked Sarah politely, in the modulated voice that her mother trained.

" Yes, she did," exclaimed Mary. " She was along with the load. Why, where is Persill ? "

This inquiry at once became general. Priscilla was nowhere in the house. The panic-stricken company could not remember seeing her since crossing the Feeder. They all thought she returned to the sled with them. John Davis was sure he helped her in.

Theophilus Gill, turning livid around the edges of his beard, said the horses might have gone to Jericho for all of him, and he 'd 'tended to Persilla Thompson himself if he had known the rest of the boys was n't goin' to. Priscilla's sister began to cry aloud, and such young ladies as did not accompany her gazed at each other in pale apprehension. But Mrs. Macauley came sternly to the front. She would not allow Mary Thompson to proclaim that Priscilla was drowned, and Theoph Gill had done it, and she forbade the party falling into a panic.

Her son Martin had his filly and sleigh ready, and while she snatched blankets and brandy, she marshaled forth such young men to form a separate search party as seemed suitable in her eyes. Mrs. Macauley would not have Priscilla Thompson drowned in the Feeder, and left strict orders on her own offspring against any such impression — which the whole company obeyed. Then she got into the sleigh, and Mart galloped his filly.

He made but one remark to his mother during this ride.

"If she'd come along with us as *I* wanted her to, this would n't have happened, . mother!"

His face showed ghastly through the dark, and his husky voice jarred the breast of the woman who bore him.

The sleigh and the sled containing the young men both stopped at that unused bridge standing in the midst of the Feeder. They all called Priscilla's name, the winter night's stillness magnifying the sound. And for reply they had a void of silence.

Mart was for dropping into the hole and searching under the ice, but his mother sternly restrained him. She sent the young men down stream, and she walked across the bridge with her son, separating from him afterward that they might search the woods in different directions.

Down the Feeder, men's voices raised melancholy echoes — "Persilla! Hoo-o-o, Persil-la! Persilla Thompson!"

The solemn winter woods could not daunt Mrs. Macauley. She gave no nervous start at twigs snapping under the snow-crust, but searched large spaces with vigor. It did hurt her to hear Mart calling the girl in such a tone, and to remember what he had said to his mother. In those days people weighed their words, and every sentence meant something. Martin's slight reproach to Mrs. Macauley was the first he had ever uttered.

Treading among naked saplings, with now and then a ghostly pawpaw leaf rustling against her face, she came to the bark sugar-house, and met Mart at its open side, carrying Priscilla in his arms. Priscilla was too terrified and exhausted to speak aloud, having crept out of the Feeder as far as this shelter. Icicles hung to her clothing, and she had lost her bonnet and cloak cape. She clung around Mrs. Macauley's neck, crying like a baby, and very unlike the dignified young woman that her small circle had always considered her. Perhaps this softness had its effect on a nature bent on commanding and protecting.

In half an hour the young folks at Macauley's knew that Mart's mother brought
Priscilla home on her lap, wrapped in blankets, and dosed with brandy every few rods.
The searchers in the sled, arriving but little
later, said Priscilla must have been clear
under the ice by the looks of it where she
crept out. But the Feeder was so shallow
right there that she could walk on the bottom.

All festivity remained suspended while
the hostess, like some mysterious medicine-
woman, worked over her patient. A few
groups in the dining-room played " fist'ock,"
and other very mild sitting diversions which
could be suspended in an instant, the play-
ers looking up with concern to receive the
latest bulletin from Priscilla.

But she recovered so rapidly that every
spirit rose, as did the general opinion of
Mrs. Macauley's skill. John Davis remarked staidly to Darius Macauley that he
believed Darius's mother knew more about
doctorin' horses, even, than most of the

horse doctors in the country, but Darius replied with some grimness, she wasn't settin'
up for that.

Finally Priscilla was able to come downstairs, holding to Mart's arm, and helped on
the other side by his mother, and everybody
said they entered the dining-room like a
bridal couple about to stand up, for she was
pale and handsome enough to be a bride,
and he looked scared and anxious enough to
be a groom. Priscilla made the effort to
come down, not only because Mrs. Macauley
considered her sufficiently restored to do so,
but also because she did not want to check
the merriment of the party.

They put her in a large chair against one
of the central posts, and Sarah Macauley, as
soon as she could catch breath for surprise,
exclaimed, loud enough to be heard by all
around her, though fortunately not by the
head of the family : —

" Why, mother ! you 've put that flowered
silk dress on her that father brought you
from Philadelphia when he went over the

mountains with a drove of horses! You
said you was goin' to save that for the oldest son's wife."

The guests near Sarah looked significantly
at each other, and Miss Miller, being among
them, tossed her head and tittered.

" Anybody who was *anxious* to marry
into your family," she remarked to Sarah,
" ought to fall sick and send for your mother, and give her all the trouble in the
world. That's the surest way to get her
consent."

Miss Miller pursed her lips. She wanted
to correct any impression that she had fa-
vored Mart Macauley, and at the same time
utter a few strictures.

" Yes, mother's a good nurse," said Sarah
innocently.

" She'll nurse *you*," whispered Darius,
with a warning nudge, " when she hears
what you said about that flowered silk."

" Don't tell her," begged his sister.   " I 'll
do your share of the milkin' all the rest of
the week, if you won't."

" Well," assented Darius provisionally,
" mebby I won't."

The flowered silk had been constructed
for Mrs. Macauley when she was much less
matronly in shape than on this Christmas
night, and by reason of being put away so
long had got into fashion again. It was so
rich and thick that it was famed through
the neighborhood as being able to stand by
itself, but, having retired to lavender and
camphor, was not expected forth any more
until the occasion of Mart Macauley's infair
dinner.

Priscilla never looked so pretty as she did
on this Christmas night. She took no part
in the plays, but they sold pawns over her
head, and the penalties she inflicted were
considered brilliant.

" Heavy, heavy, what hangs over your
head!" said John Davis, the seller, holding
Miss Miller's real gold ring. Her father
had tried that ring with aquafortis before
he allowed her to buy it of the peddler.

"Is it fine or superfine?" inquired Priscilla.

"Superfine," said John, pulling his neck-erchief with an air. "What must be done to redeem it?"

"Let the owner make a charade."

This sent Miss Miller, with assistants, giggling into the pantry. And a grand charade they exhibited, for Miss Miller had picked up such things among the Lancaster young people, and was not sorry to show her knowledge. First the actors came in supporting each other and weeping aloud. In their second act there were several dumb weddings, and in their third the weddings were repeated with a change of partners. After long guessing, everybody was struck with admiration to discover that the word was Bal-ti-more.

Then John sold Martin's big handker-chief over Priscilla's head, informing her it was fine only. And the possessor was bid to bow to the wittiest, kneel to the prettiest, and kiss the one he loved best, which Mar-tin did, perambulating about the room in a long search, but coming back to Priscilla in every instance, covering her with confusion, and exciting the company to hilarity.

Mrs. Macauley having discreetly retired, they played "London Bridge is swept away," furnishing the music with their own voices. The figures and changes made it very similar to the "Virginia Reel," and Mrs. Macauley would have thought it sounded like a dance had she not known "London Bridge," to be an innocent marching play.

Supper was served at ten o'clock, with plates and white-handled knives and forks held upon the knee, this variety of refreshment being called a lap supper. The Macauley genius for cookery shone resplendent. Such cold meats and pickles and spiced breads, such coffee (made at a neighboring house in a wash-boiler, by Mrs. Macauley, just before she retired), such varieties of cake and pie, such metheglin and root beer, flowed upon the guests as only Macauleys knew how to make and brew.

"You don't seem to be havin' as good a time as the rest," observed Philip Welchammer to Theophilus Gill, when the plates were being collected, and his plate retained a pile of scarcely touched dainties.

" Oh, I 'm gittin' along, I 'm gittin' along," said Theophilus.

" You 'pear kind o' sober."

" Well, 't was a scare," apologized Theophilus.

" But that 's all over now."

" Yes, it 's all over," assented the black-bearded lover, with a sigh. And plucking up animation, he added, " Mart has kind o' took the bit in his teeth, hain't he ? "

" He has that. It 's a match now, if Persilla 's a mind to have him. The old lady, she 's turned round and set herself that way too. I should n't be surprised if the 's an infair to this house by next Chris'mas."

" No, neither would I," said Theophilus, shaking his head, and making a grimace as if the action hurt him. He had a stirring, money-making disposition, while Mart Macauley's tastes were those of a student, and he thought himself as good a match. But there was no accounting for the tricks of fate.

Philip laughed in a heartening and sympathetic fashion.

"I reckon the' won't be no chance for you next Sunday night, nor any other Sunday night this year, now," he said.

"Mebby not," said Theophilus. "But if Mart Macauley gits her, he gits the Queen of the Swamp, sure as you 're born. She 'll always be that, come what will."

THE STIRRING-OFF

TIME, 1850

DAVIS's boys said to all the young men at singing-school, " Come over to 'r sugar-camp Saturday night; we 're goin' to stir off."

The young men, sitting on the fence to which horses were tied in dusky rows, play-fully imitated the preacher when he gave out appointments, and replied they would be there, no preventing Providence, at early candle-lighting.

Jane Davis, attended by her cousin, also circulated among the girls in the school-house during that interval in singing-school called recess, and invited them to the stir-ring-off.

The Davises, though by no means the rich-est, were the most hospitable family in the Swamp. They came from Virginia. Their

stable swarmed with fine horses, each son
and daughter owning a colt; and the steeds
of visiting neighbors often crowded the stalls
until these looked like a horse-fair.

The Davises entertained every day in the
year. Their house was unpretending even
for those times, being of unpainted wood,
with a bedroom at each side of the porch, a
sitting-room where guns and powder-horns
hung over the fireplace, a kitchen, and a
loft. Yet here sojourned relations from
other counties, and even from over the mountains. Here on Christmas and New Year's
days were made great turkey-roasts. Out
of it issued Jane Davis to the dances and
parties where she was a belle, and her brothers, ruddy, huge-limbed, black-eyed, and
dignified as any young men in Fairfield
County.

They kept bees, and raised what were
called noble turnips. Their farm appeared
to produce solely for the use of guests. In
watermelon season they kept what might be

termed open field. Their cookery was celebrated, and their cordiality as free as sunshine. No unwelcome guest could alight at
Davis's. The head of the family, Uncle
Davis was a "general," and this title carried as much social weight as that of judge.
About their premises hung an atmosphere
of unending good times. On Sunday afternoons late in November all the raw young
men of the neighborhood drew in a circle to
Davis's fireplace, scraping turnips or apples.
Now the steel knives moved in concert, and
now they jarred; the hollow wall of a tur-
nip protested against the scrape, and Aunt
Davis passed the heaping pan again. Or
cracked walnuts and hickory nuts were the
offerings. Then every youth sat with an
overflowing handkerchief on his lap, and the
small blade of his knife busy with the ker-
nels, — backlog and forestick being bom-
barded with shells which burned in blue and
crimson.

So when the Davises were ready to stir

off in their sugar-camp, it was the most natural thing in the world for them to invite their neighbors to come and eat the sugar, and for their neighbors to come and do so.

The camp threw its shine far among leafless trees. Three or four iron kettles steamed on a pole over the fire. In a bark lodge near by, Aunt Davis had put a lunch of pies and cakes before she went home, to be handed around at the stirring-off. It was a clear starry night, the withered sod crisp underfoot with the stiffness of ice. Any group approaching silently could hear the tapped maples dripping a liquid nocturne into trough or pan.

But scarcely any groups approached silently. They were heard chatting in the open places, and their calls raised echoes.

John and Eck Davis had collected logs and chunks and spread robes and blankets until the seating capacity of the camp was nearly equal to that of George's Chapel.

Some of the girls took off their wraps and hung them in the bark house. One couple carried away a bucket for more sugar-water to cool a kettle, and other couples sauntered after them. There were races on the spongy dead leaves, and sudden squalls of remonstrance.

Jane Davis stood in the midst of her company, moving a long wooden stirrer in the kettle about to sugar-off. Though her beauty was neither brown nor white, nor, in fact, positive beauty of any kind, it cajoled everybody. Her hair was folded close to her cheeks. There was innocent audacity in the curving line of every motion she made. The young men were so taken by the spell of her grace that she was accused of being unrighteously engaged to three at once, and about to add her cousin Tom Randall to the list.

Tom Randall was a Virginian, spending the winter in Ohio. He was handsome, merry as Mercutio, and so easy in his man-

ners that the Swamp youths watched him
with varying emotions. He brought his
songs over the mountains: one celebrated
the swiftness of the electric telegraph in
flashing news from Baltimore to Wheeling;
another was about a Quaker courtship, and
set all the Swamp girls to rattling the lady's
brisk response, —

> " What care I for your rings or money, —
> Faddle-a-ding, a-ding, a-day ;
> I want a man that will call me honey, —
> Faddle-a-ding, a-ding, a-day ! "

Tom Randall sat close to the fire, hanging
his delicate hands, which had never done a
day's chopping, over his knees. He looked
much of a gentleman, Nora Waddell remarked aside to Philip Welchammer. To
all the girls he was a central figure, as Jane
was a central figure to the young men.

But Philip claimed that Virginians were
no nearer perfection than out-and-out Swamp
fellows.

" I didn't say he was a perfect gentle·

man," said Nora, with cautious moderation,
"for I would n't say so of any man."

"He ain't proud," admitted Philip.
"He's free to talk with everybody."

"Humph!" remarked Mary Thompson,
sitting at the other side of Philip; "he
ought to be. Folks in Georger Chapel
neighborhood is just as good as anybody."

"Well, anyhow, I know he ain't a prettier dancer than Jane," sighed Nora, whose
folks would not allow her to indulge in the
godless motion which the music of a fiddle
inspires. While Jane stirred and chatted,
she was swaying and taking dance-steps, as
if unable to refrain from spinning away
through the trees. In this great woods
drawing-room, where so many were gathered,
it was impossible for her to hear any com-
ment that went on.

"Jane makes a good appearance on the
floor," responded Philip, who, being male,
could withstand the general denunciations
of the preacher and his mother's praying at

him in meeting. "I like to lead her out to dance."

"Uncle and Aunt Davis are just as easy with Jane as if they was n't perfessors of religion," sighed Nora Waddell.

"And their boys thinks so much of her," added Mary Thompson. "John can't go anywhere unless she ties his neck-han'ketcher for him. I've knowed him, when Jane was sick, to come and lean over her to get it fixed."

"If she's to leave them," said Philip, "I wonder how they'd do without her?"

"She's goin' to marry Cousin Jimmy Thompson, that I know," said Mary.

"She's engaged to Dr. Miller in Lancaster," insisted Nora. "I've saw voluntines he's sent her."

"Dick Hanks thinks he's goin' to get her," laughed Philip. "He told me she's as good as promised him. And Dick's a good feller, if he was n't such a coward."

"I don't believe Jane wants anybody,"

said Nora Waddell. "She's light-minded, and likes to enjoy herself."

Dick Hanks stood by Jane and insisted on helping her to move the stirrer. His hair inclosed his head in the shape of a thatch, leaving but narrow eaves of forehead above his eyebrows, though his expression was open and amiable. He looked like one of Bewick's cuts of an English carter. The Hankses, however, were a rich family, and, in spite of their eccentricities, a power in the county. Old Jimmy Hanks so dreaded the grave that he had a marble vault hewed, watching its progress for years, and getting himself ready to occupy it a few weeks after its completion. Lest he should be buried alive, his will decreed that the vault should be unlocked and the coffin examined at intervals. The sight of a face floating in alcohol and spotted with drops from the metal casket not proving grateful to his heirs, the key was soon conveniently lost.

His son Dick, hearty in love and friend-

ship and noble in brawn, so feared the dark
that he would not go into an unlighted
room. When left by himself at the parting
of roads after a night's frolic, he galloped
his horse through brush and mire, and it
was told that he had more than once reached
home without a whole stitch to his back.

But in spite of the powers of darkness,
Dick was anxious to take Jane Davis under
his protection. The fire and the noisy company kept him from lifting his eyes to the
treetops swaying slowly overhead, and the
lonesome stars. All through the woods win-
ter-night sounds and sudden twig cracklings
could be heard. Dick, however, meant to
take Jane Davis home, whether he could
persuade one of the Davis boys to go home
with him afterward or not.

In those days neighborhoods were intensely
local. The people knew what historians
have not yet learned about the value of
isolated bits of human life. These young
folks in the sugar-camp knew nothing of

the events and complications of the great
world, but they all felt more or less inter-
ested in the politics of Jane Davis's entan-
glements.

Her brother kept dipping a long spoon
into the kettle she stirred, and dropping the
liquid into a tin cup of cold sugar-water.
As long as the hot stuff twined about in
ropy arms, it was syrup; but as soon as it
settled to the bottom in a clear mass, it was
wax, and the change from wax to the grain
of sugar is a sudden one.

When Eck Davis announced, " It 's
waxed," the kettle was slung off in haste,
and everybody left the tree which had
propped his back, or the robe on which he
had leaned, and the graining sugar was
served in saucers and handed around. It
could be eaten with spoons or " worked "
into crackling ropes. Davis's boys took off
the syrup kettles and covered them up in
the bark lodge. They would be emptied
into stone jars when the more important

business of entertaining company was over. The fire now shone redder. Jane was cutting up pies and cakes in the bark house, all this warm light focused on her lowered eyelids, when more of her suitors arrived.

"I knowed the entire posse would be out," said Philip Welchammer in a laughing undertone to the girls sitting beside him. "Davises never misses invitin' anybody."

"You're too late, Jimmy Thompson," called Jane's elder brother before he noticed the preacher was in the party. "Your sheer's e't." When, however, Dr. Miller from Lancaster also came forward, John stood up stiffly and put on his company grandeur. He held the town-man in some awe, and was bound to be constrained by the preacher.

Jimmy Thompson, having met Jane with awkward heartiness, said he would make the young folks acquainted with Brother Gurley. They all knew Brother Gurley; but Jimmy was a wild young man, and his audacity in

" brother "-ing the preacher was more delicious than home-made sugar. He afterward
explained that the preacher had been turned
onto the old folks for Sunday, and he asked
him along to the frolic without suspicionin'
he'd come, but the preacher, he took a-holt
as if that was the understandin'.

Jane met Brother Gurley and Dr. Miller
with equal ease. A hush fell upon the company, and they ate and watched her serve
the newcomers and appear to balance such
formidable individuals in her hands. Affec-
tation was in that region the deadliest sin a
girl could commit against her own popular-
ity, and Jane's manner was always beautifully simple.

The preacher had a clean-shaven, large
face, huge blue eyes, and laughing white
teeth, and a sprinkling of fine, indefinitely
tinted hair. His figure was vigorous, and
well made to bear the hardships of a Methodist circuit-rider. His presence had the
grasp of good-fellowship and power, and

rather dwarfed Dr. Miller, whom all the girls thought a very pretty man. Dr. Miller wore side-whiskers, and a Lancaster suit of clothes finished by a fine round cloak hooked under his chin. When he took off his hat to bow, two curls fell over his forehead. The woman who would not take Dr. Miller if he wanted her must expect to have the pick of creation, and maybe she would miss it after all. He talked to Jane and ate maple sugar with the greatest of Lancaster ease, telling her he had put up with his cousin in Millersport and borrowed a horse to ride to camp. John Davis at once said the folks at home expected him to put up with them over Sunday, and the other young men resented the doctor's prompt acceptance of Davis's hospitality.

The preacher, holding his saucer of sugar in his left hand, was going around and giving the right hand of fellowship to every young person in camp. This was the proper and customary thing for him to do. A

preacher who went into company anywhere
on the circuit without shaking hands and
pushing and strengthening his acquaintance
would be a worse stumbling-block than a
backslider given up to superfluous clothing
and all kinds of sinful levity, or a new
convert with artificials in her bonnet. But
there was a tingling quality in Brother
Gurley's grasp which stirred the blood;
and his heavy voice was as prevailing in its
ordinary tones as in the thunders of the
pulpit.

" Did you bring your wife with you, Brother Gurley? " simpered Tabitha Gill, a
dwarfish, dark old maid, devout in church
and esteemed for her ability to make a good
prayer.

Mary Thompson whispered behind her
back, " Tabitha Gill's always for findin' out
whether a preacher's married or not before
anybody else does."

" Not this time," replied Brother Gurley,
warming Sister Gill's heart with a broad,

class-meeting smile. "But I expect to bring her with me when I come around again."

"Do," said Tabitha; "and stop at our house."

"I'm obliged to you, Sister Gill," replied the preacher. "You have a fine community of young people here."

"But they ain't none of 'em converted. There's a good deal of levity in Georger Chapel neighborhood. Now, Jane, now, — Jane Davis, — she's a girl nobody can help likin', but many's the night that she's danced away in sinful amusement. I wish you'd do somethin' for her soul, Brother Gurley."

"I'll try," responded the preacher heartily. He looked with a tender and indulgent eye at Jane, who was dividing her company into two parts, to play one innocent play before the camp broke up.

"Come away from here," whispered Philip Welchammer to the girl beside him, seceding from the preacher's group and adding himself to Jane's. "Tabitha Gill will be haulin' us all up to the mourners' bench pretty soon."

They played "clap-out," the girls sitting in their wraps all ready to depart, and the young men turning up their collars and tying on their comforters while waiting a summons. Jane was leader, and with much tittering and secrecy each young lady imparted to Jane the name of the youth she wished to have sit beside her. Dick Hanks was called first, and he stood looking at the array from which he could take but one choice, his lips dropping apart and his expression like that he used to display under the dunce-cap at Gum College. During this interval of silence the drip of sugar-water into troughs played a musical phrase or two, and the stirring and whinnying of the horses could be heard where they were tied to saplings. No rural Ohioan ever walked a quarter of a mile if he had any kind of beast or conveyance to carry him.

Then Dick of course sat down by the wrong girl, and was clapped out, and Dr. Miller was called. Dr. Miller made a pleasing impression by hesitating all along the line, and when he sat down by Mary Thompson her murmur of assent was a tribute to his sagacity. Cousin Tom Randall was summoned, and sung two or three lines of the " Quaker's Courtship " before throwing himself on the mercy of Nora Waddell. He was clapped out, and said he always expected it. West of the Alleghanies was no place for him; they were even goin' to clap him out up at uncle's. Then the preacher came smiling joyfully, and placed himself by Tabitha Gill, where he was tittered over and allowed to remain; and one by one the seats were filled, the less fortunate men making a second trial with more success when their range was narrowed.

Everybody rose up to go home. But a great many " good-nights," and reproaches for social neglect, and promises of future devotion to each other, had first to be exchanged. Then Jimmy Thompson, who had driven in his buggy expressly to take Jane Davis home, and was wondering what he should do with the preacher, saw with astonishment that Brother Gurley had Jane upon his own arm and was tucking her shawl close to her chin. Her black eyes sparkled within a scarlet hood. She turned about with Brother Gurley, facing all the young associates of her life, and said, " We want you all to come to our house after preachin' to-morrow. The presidin' elder will be there."

" I don't care nothin' about the presidin' elder," muttered Jimmy Thompson.

" Goin' to be a weddin', you know," explained John Davis, turning from assisting his brother Eck to empty the syrup kettles, and beaming warmly over such a general occasion. " The folks at meeting will all be invited, but Jane said she wanted to ask the young people separate to-night."

" And next time I come around the circuit," said Brother Gurley, gathering Jane's
hand in his before the company, " I 'll bring
my wife with me."

They walked away from the campfire,
Jane turning her head once or twice to call
" Good-night, all," as if she still clung to
every companionable hand. The party
watched her an instant in silence. Perhaps
some were fanciful enough to see her walking away from the high estate of a doctor's
wife in Lancaster, from the Hanks money,
and Jimmy Thompson's thrift, into the constant change and unfailing hardships of
Methodist itinerancy. The dancing motion
would disappear from her gait, and she who
had tittered irreverently at her good mother's
labors with backsliders at the mourners'
bench would come to feel an interest in such
sinners herself.

" Dog 'd if I thought Jane Davis would
ever marry a preacher! " burst out Jimmy
Thompson, in sudden and hot disapproval.

" Don't it beat all ! " murmured Tabitha Gill. " And her an unconverted woman in the error of her ways! Jane's too young for a preacher's wife."

, " Jane's fooled us all," owned Philip Welchammer heartily. To keep intended nuptials a family secret until a day or a few hours before the appointed time was as much a custom of the country as was prying into and spying out such affairs. Surprising her friends by her wedding was, therefore, adding to Jane's social successes ; but only Dr. Miller could perceive her true reason for assembling her suitors at the last moment. While discarding them all, her hospitable nature clung to their friendship ; she wished to tell them in a group the change she contemplated, so that no one could accuse her of superior kindness to another. Her very cruelties were intended mercies.

" That's the way the pretty girls go," sighed Cousin Tom Randall, seizing hold of Jane's younger brother : " the preachers get 'em. Come on, Eck ; I have to be helped home."

" I don't see when he courted her," breathed Dick Hanks, closing his lips after many efforts.

" Preachers is chain-lightnin'," laughed Jimmy Thompson. " He 's been around often enough, and always stoppin' there."

" To-morrow after preachin'," said John impressively, as he came forward after hastily covering the jars. " We 're goin' to have a turkey-dinner, and we want you all to be sure to come. And next time Brother Gurley and Jane makes the circuit, we 'll have the infair at our house, too."

" That 's just like Davises," exclaimed one of the dispersing group in the midst of their eager promises ; " they would n't be satisfied unless they give the weddin' and the infair both, and invited all quarterly meetin' to set down to the table. I thought there was doin 's over at their house ; but then they 're always bakin' and fussin'.'"

They could all picture a turkey-roast at
Davis's : the crisp, brown turkeys rising
from their own dripping, squares of pone as
yellow as buttercups, and biscuits calculated
to melt whitely with honey from glass dishes
of sweet-smelling combs. There would be
every kind of vegetable grown in the Swamp,
and game from the banks of the Feeder and
Reservoir, pies and cakes and coffee, and at
least eight kinds of preserves. Jane Davis
and the preacher would stand up in front of
the fireplace, and after the ceremony there
would be a constant rattle of jokes from the
presiding elder and his assistants. And
over the whole house would hang that happy ·
atmosphere which makes one think of corn
ripening on a sunny hillside in still September weather. A dozen times the long tables
would be replenished and supplied with
plates, all the usual features of a turkey-
roast at Davis's being exaggerated by the
importance of the occasion ; and Aunt Davis
would now and then forget to urge a guest,

while she hurriedly wiped her eyes and replied to some expression of neighborly sympathy, that they had to lose Jane some time, and it was a good thing for a girl to get a religious man. Then about dusk the preachers and their congregation would start again to chapel, and Jane, in Millersport clothes, would shine on the front seats as a bride, certain of an ovation when the after-meeting handshaking came. It would be a spite if she sat where tallow candles could drip on her from one of the wooden chandeliers, but she would enjoy hearing her bridegroom exhort, and he would feel like exhorting with all his might.

" Well, Doc," said John Davis, turning from the deserted camp and sinking fire to place himself by the bridle of the young man from Lancaster.

" No," answered Dr. Miller, " I 'm obliged to you, John ; but I 'll ride back to Millersport to-night."

" You don't feel put out ? " urged John,

conscious of a pang because all the good fellows who courted Jane could not become his brothers-in-law.

" No ; oh, no," protested Dr. Miller with chagrin. " She 'd a right to suit herself. I 'll be around some other day."

" We 'd take it hard if you did n't," said John.

" But just now," concluded the doctor, " I feel what a body might call — stirred-off."

Dick Hanks was riding up close to Jimmy Thompson, while Jimmy unblanketed his mare and prepared for a deliberate departure.

" John, now," remarked Jimmy, — " he brothered the preacher right up, did n't he ? They 'll be makin' a class-leader o' John yet, if they can git him to quit racin' horses."

" Which way you goin' home, Jimmy ? " inquired Dick Hanks anxiously.

" The long way, round by Georger Chapel, where I can look at the tombstones for company. Want to go along? We can talk over the weddin', and you're only two mile from home at our woods' gate."

"I guess I'll take the short cut through the brush," said Dick.

Jimmy drove through the clearing and fence-gap, where John Davis was waiting to lay up the rails again.

"What's that?" said John, and they both paused to listen.

It was a sound of crashing and scampering, of smothered exclamation and the rasping and tearing of garments. Dick Hanks was whipping his steed through the woods, against trees, logs, and branches, as if George's Chapel graveyard, containing the ghastly vault of his father, and George's Chapel preacher, waving Jane Davis in one victorious hand, were both in merciless pursuit of him.

SWEETNESS

Time, 1855

Amber light in the dense Ohio woods re-
ceded slowly from the path which a woman
ascended. The earth was frozen, and glazed
puddles stood in cow tracks. But this woman loved to climb from the valley farms
and her day's sewing, of chill December
evenings, and feel that she approached her
heaven and left the world behind. The year
had just passed its shortest day. Neighborhood custom allowed her to leave her tasks
early in the evening, because she came to
· them with a lantern in the morning. She
hastened as you may have noticed a large-
eyed anxious cow cantering toward its nurs-
ling; but stopped to breathe, half ashamed
of herself, in sight of a log-house known
through the Rocky Fork settlement as
Coon's.

All the Coons had been queer little people, but this last daughter of them exceeded
her forefathers in squatty squareness of stature and Japanese cast of feature. As she
was quite thirty-five her friends called her
an old maid, according to the custom of that
remote period. Yet there was not a girl on
all the windings of the Rocky Fork who had
more laughter in her eyes, or smoother
cheeks, or darker polished hair.

"Sure's my name is Wilda Coon," said
the small woman beneath her breath, "yonder comes Lanson Bundle."

The man she saw was yet far off, plodding
across the valley toward her hillside; and as
he had taken that walk nearly every evening
for a dozen years, it should have ceased to
surprise her. Yet as shadows thickened ·
among rock and naked trees, it was always
a satisfaction to turn and look back from
that particular point and exclaim, "Yonder
comes Lanson Bundle!"

Wilda's log-house had a clearing and

some acres of trees around it, standing like a German principality or an oasis in the midst of Alanson Bundle's great farm. The Bundles had vainly tried in times past to buy out the Coons. But Alanson had other views. He had courted Wilda twelve years, and he calculated in time to wear her out. She could not go on forever raising patches of truck in the summer, and quilting and sewing in the winter.

Alanson was not uncomfortable while he waited. His aunt kept house for him at his homestead, where he had several barns, a milk-house, a smoke-house and all modern conveniences around him. He felt his value with everybody but Wilda. The youngest girls showed him no discouragement. There was a sonorous pomp about his singing in meeting which affected every rural nature, while his Adam's apple, like a sensitive lump of mercury, trembled up and down its inclosure. Some folks thought Alanson Bundle ought to have been a preacher. He would look so nice standing in a pulpit, with his hair sleeked up in a straight roach, saying, " Hence we discover, my brethren." But Wilda Coon never had made any fuss over him. And for that reason he followed her with abject service.

In that early year of the fifties a great many people about the Rocky Fork had locks on their doors. But a tow latch-string hung out for Wilda Coon, and with it she lifted the wooden latch of her dwelling. At night, for security, she would draw the string inside, and slip a wooden bar into staples across the thick board portal.

The tight-chinked cabin had the strangest interior on the Rocky Fork. There was only one room, and the hollow of the roof rose up in a cavernous arch without joists. Two wooden bars were, indeed, set high across one corner, but they served as roosts for chickens who had already taken to them for the night, and who stirred quavering as Wilda shut the door and emptied a gourd.

Before the fire, yet not too near it, was a trundle-bed which could be pushed anywhere on wheels.

She dropped her hood and shawl upon a chair and slipped toward the trundle-bed, motioning back a great mastiff who kept guard at the hearth. He sat down again and licked his lips; the· glory of burning logs in the fireplace was enough to content any dog, for that cabin seemed to have the sunset imprisoned within it. Calico curtains on the four-paned windows hid darkening woods outside.

" O Sweetness ! " whispered Wilda, bending over the trundle-bed and scarcely daring to touch the patchwork quilt. Her eyes were full of kisses and fondling for her only baby, the helpless being who reversed for her the maternal relations. It was a little old woman, whose apple face had shriveled into puckers only around the corners of the eyes and mouth. A dimity nightcap tied it in, almost covering white silk threads of hair. This helpless mother, lying in the dead alive state we now call paralysis, and the Rocky Forkers then called palsy, was the secret delight of Wilda's heart, and Alanson Bundle's only rival. But she concealed her fondness like a crime. The name of Sweetness was sacred to that hollow cabin. Bounce could make no remark about it, and he was the only safe auditor in an age when excess of loving was considered weakness.

Wilda hung her supper kettles on the hooks of the crane, and made biscuits, and raked out coals to bake them in a Dutch oven. Alanson Bundle would not appear until the evening meal was over. He pottered around in his woods or went across the ridge to look after cattle.

The log-house was exquisite with cleanness, even in that corner where the fowls roosted. No cobwebs or dust marred the rich brown of its upper depth. The floor and stone hearth were scoured white. Wilda's spinning-wheel stood beside one wall. Her own apartment was an oblong space curtained with homespun which had been dyed a dull red. Some red and gilt chairs, a pine table and a red and gilt cushioned settee on rockers, furnished the house. The log wall between hearth and door held gay trappings of tinware and pewter, all shining in the mighty blaze.

The table was spread and a perfume of coffee filled the place. Wilda had turned the fried eggs and lifted them carefully to a platter before she heard the usual sounds her mother made to call her.

Sweetness was wide awake and smiling like a baby. The Rocky Fork people said she had her faculties but could n't make no use of them. Unabated intelligence looked through her eyes and her face never distorted itself, although she could not talk.

" Have you been lonesome to-day, Sweetness? No? Have you slept much? Yes? That's good. Did Speckle and Banty sit

on Bounce's back and keep you company?
They've gone to roost now. They're going
to wake up about midnight and crow for
Christmas, and wake you up — the bad
chickens. — Now supper's ready. Folks
round here thinks I starve you because you
never eat in the middle of the day. 'T ain't
no use for me to say anything. But if you
don't want me to be clean disgraced, you
must eat hearty when you do eat."

She fed the helpless being with long and
patient use of a spoon. The fire roared.
Bounce rose up and yawned, stretching his
limbs, to hint that his own plate had been
empty since morning. But Wilda never
hurried this important part of her day's
business. The food which she must eat became overdone. She sat on the trundle-bed,
giving her mother with the spoon meat all
the life and doings of that small world on
the Rocky Fork.

" Gutteridges were going to have a turkey-
roast to-morrow. The presiding elder was

at their house. Yes, their sewing was done; she finished Mandy's black quilted petticoat to-day. Mandy and 'Lizabeth both had new shawls that their father had paid six dollars apiece for, at the woolen factory in Newark; stripes and crossbars. Ridenour's little boy was so he could sit up; the doctor thought the fever was broke. The Bankses were all going to take dinner at granny's. And some folks said one of Harris's girls was to be married to-morrow, but it might be all talk. There was n't much chance of snow, but it was a cold night outside. Did n't Sweetness hear the wind across the roof? It was a good thing our clapboards were on so tight."

So this one-sided conversation went on until the little old woman was quite filled. Then Wilda made her snug, as if attending an infant, and fed Bounce, and sat down alone at the table:

Scarcely were the clean pewter and crockery in place again, and the wheel set out where the table had been, and Wilda bundled ready to go out, when a knock sounded on the door.

She opened it, and exclaimed as she always did, —

"Well, I declare! here's Lanson. Come in, Lanson, and take a chair."

"Gimme your milk bucket," responded Alanson.

"I was just starting to milk, Lanson. Don't you bother yourself with it to-night."

But he took her pail. And Wilda, smiling, laid off her wraps and made the hearth very clean, and plumped up the settee cushions.

When Alanson handed the frothing pail into the door, without putting foot over the threshold, he glanced at the fireplace.

"Want another log brought in to-night?"

"Law, Lanson! that one ain't half burnt."

"But it'll settle down before another twenty-four hours. I 'low I'd better fetch a few sticks."

So he came in laden with sections of

trees, and built them handily upon the structure of the fire.

" Do you want ary bucket of water?" was his next inquiry.

" No, I'm obleeged to you, Lanson," replied Wilda. " I fetched a big gourdful from the spring as I come uphill. It saves steps."

Alanson now unbelted and took off his butternut-colored wamus, and Wilda hung it with his hat on a peg. He had a fine black blanket shawl for meeting, but he was not so reckless as to scratch it through hill underbrush every evening.

Feeling himself now ready for society, Alanson walked over to the trundle-bed and greeted the invalid.

" Good even', Mis' Coon ; it's right wintry outdoors."

She gave him an approving smile. He sat down in the settee and rocked himself, while Wilda pulled a long thread from her spindle, stepped back and gave the wheel a

whirl. The trundle-bed, as usual, stood between her and her besieger. A hum, rising
and rising like some sweet tune through the
pines, filled the room. The great wheel
blurred all its spokes, and found them again,
and slackened to a slow revolution, as Wilda
came back to the spindle.

"How's your aunt to-day?" she inquired.

"Middling," replied Alanson. Again the
music of the spinning arose. Alanson
warmed his feet and hands, and felt comforted after his tramp through the vast chill
woods.

When the silent companionship which he
enjoyed with Wilda had quite filled its mea-
sure, he took from his pocket and unfolded
a large newspaper.

"I'll light a candle," said Wilda, with
that eagerness for romance which the sim-
plest lives manifest.

"'T isn't needed," said Alanson. What
was a candle's star to that blazing sun in
the fireplace? He turned his shoulder so

the light fell upon the " Saturday Evening Post," and read a harrowing installment about some Bride of the Wilderness. There was domestic bliss in this snug cabin, the wind-song of the wheel, and the winter night with its breath of Christmas. Alanson droned on in a high key, the mother watching him as long as she was able to resist so many monotones. She went to sleep before Wilda's stint of spinning was done, and before Alanson read with impressive voice, " To be con-tin-u-ed."

That wary inspection of each other which people of that time called courting had varied its routine so little for twelve years betwixt this pair, that Alanson felt bound to make his usual remark as Wilda sat down to knit.

" Well, folks is still talking about us getting married, Wilda."

" Let them talk," said Wilda, putting her hair behind her ear, and smiling while she looked at Sweetness.

" I come here pretty regular. Don't you think it's about time we set the day?"

Wilda answered, without moving her eyes from the trundle-bed, " Don't you think we better let well enough alone, Lanson?"

" Well, now, 't is n't well enough," argued Alanson, and to the sylvan mind there is accumulated force in an oft-used argument. " You 've got these woods lots and the house and a cow" —

" Yes, I 'm well fixed," murmured Wilda.

— " but you have to leave your mother and go out among the neighbors to airn a living. How do you know sometime the house won't burn down?"

" I am jub'ous about it often," owned Wilda, biting the end of a knitting-needle. But catching the yarn over her little finger she drove it ahead with her work.

" Then eventually she might die."

" I 've thought of that," sighed Wilda. " And I 've thought what 'd become of her if I 's to be taken and her left. Then who 'd let her pet rooster and hen — that she's just as tickled with as a child — roost in the house, and clean after them without fretting her?"

Alanson glanced at Speckle and Banty sticking like balls to their perch, and he volunteered some discreet possibilities.

" When folks begins to get used to such things before they're too old and sot in their ways, seems to me like chickens in the house would be natteral enough — though not brought up to it."

Whenever Alanson made this great concession, Wilda always fell back upon her observations of marriage.

" But there's Mary Jane Willey. She had fifteen hundred dollars in her own right, and was well fixed with bedding and goods — six chairs and a bread-trough and a cupboard. And all that did n't satisfy her, but she must have a man to speckalate with her money and lose it; and now he's took to drinking, her and her children are like to go on the county."

Alanson interlaced his fingers across his chest and set his thumbs to whirling.

" She ought to got a man like me," he observed humorously.

Then the topic was usually diverted into the lives of other Rocky Forkers until Alanson felt it was time to go home.

But to-night, after drawing out his silver watch by its steel log-chain, he lingered uneasily instead of rising from the settee and saying, " Well, I better be moseying towards home."

The flashing of Wilda's needles went on. She had a leather stall pinned to her waist, in which she braced and steadied the most rampant needle as he led the gallop around the stocking. Sweetness slept as a spirit may sleep who has escaped the bounds of care, her sunken little mouth and wrinkled eye-corners steadily smiling.

" Going to have any Christmas up here to-morrow ? " inquired Alanson, with a sheepish look at Wilda.

" I got a Christmas gift for her," replied
Wilda fondly. Alanson understood the pro-
nouns which always stood for mother.

" Well, now, it 's funny," said he. " But
I got something for her, too."

" Why, Lanson! What ever put you up
to do such a thing?" Wilda paused with
her needle held back in mid plunge.

" 'T is n't much," apologized Alanson, and
he brought his wamus from the peg to the
hearth. Wilda had noticed it was laden
when she hung it up, but she always discreetly overlooked the apples he brought
until he made his offering.

There were no apples in the wamus pockets
this time. Alanson took out two packets,
and opened one which he laid on Wilda's
knee. It was a pound of red hearts.

" The other 's for her," he said " and it 's
all white ones."

" Why, Lanson Bundle! " exclaimed
Wilda.

But he had yet another paper, and it disclosed the yellow coats of tropical fruit.

"What's them?" breathed Wilda, bending over in admiration. "Why, Lanson Bundle! If them ain't lemons and oranges! Where in this world did you get them?"

"I sent clean to Fredericktown for them," confessed the suitor with an apologetic grin. "I thought her being bedfast so steady all the time, she'd like something out of the common."

"You are *real* clever," spoke Wilda with trembling voice. "She'll be so tickled! I been making her two fine caps with hemstitching around the border; — but this does beat all!"

"I done something else," Alanson ventured on, "that you'll think is simple; — I've never seen such a thing, but I've read about it. Coming along through the pines I took my jack-knife out and cut a little one off close to the ground; and it's laying outside the door."

"What for, Lanson?"

"A Christmas-tree."

" What 's that ? "

" Why, in a foreign place they call Germany, I 've read they take an evergreen and make it stand like it growed in the house, and hang gifts on it, and if I don't disremember, they fix candles into it and light them."

" I should think that would be pretty," said Wilda in some excitement. " Law, Lanson ! If we could fix it at the foot of her trundle-bed ! "

Alanson thought they could fix it, and he set vigorously about the task. He ran out to the ash-hopper and brought in the keg which in summer time caught the lye. The evergreen tree, beautifully straight, and tasseled at the top, he fastened in the keg ingeniously, without clamor of nails and pounding.

Then maid and bachelor trimmed the Christmas tree for their old sleeping child. A dexterous use of string hung all the hearts to the boughs, as well as oranges and lemons.

One cap was put on the top tassel, and the other dropped from a branch by its ties. Wilda brought out her candle box and recklessly cut the moulded tallow into short tapers. This part of the decoration greatly taxed both Alanson and her. But they finally pinned all the tapers in place, and concluded to light the wicks for a trial.

Alanson carried a brand from point to point. Wilda was frightened at the beauty of the thing and their unusual occupation. Her eyes and cheeks were vivid. She had never been so wildly excited in her life before. Thought and resolution, which had battled for years, bounded forward with the bounding of her blood,

"Lanson Bundle!" she laughed, "what do you suppose folks would say if they peeked in and seen us at this!"

" I 'low they 'd want to have a Christmas-tree themselves," responded the bachelor. "You and me will have one next year at our own house, won't we, Wilda?"

"Well, I don't know but we will. I don't know as I can hold out much longer. You're a real good man, Lanson, and if I've got to get married, there ain't nobody I'd have as quick as you."

At that admission Alanson laid the brand on the fire, wiped his lips carefully with a red cotton handkerchief, and came expectantly round the Christmas-tree. But with the recoil of a middle-aged girl from dropping man a word of encouragement, Wilda flew behind the trundle-bed and kept her lover warned by an uplifted palm.

" I have n't made up my mind to no kissing yet, Lanson Bundle! I ain't used to kissing anybody but her."

Alanson looked at the little mother in the trundle-bed, and she opened her eyes, disturbed by such scampering. The pet chickens were roused also, and Speckle crowed on his perch with a vigor which belongs only to the midnight of Christmas eve.

" Look there, Sweetness," Wilda whis-

pered kneeling. " Do you see what Lanson 's
fixed for you ?   That 's a Christmas-tree."

The mother's eyes caught the Christmas-
tree, and snapped with astonishment and delight.   The tapers were dripping tallow, but
firelight shone through the boughs, and all
the wonderful hearts and yellow fruit hung
like a fairy picture.   Her grateful look
finally sought Alanson, and he also knelt
down, at the opposite side of the trundle-bed,
and with reverence which brought a rush of
tears to Wilda's eyes, kissed Sweetness on
the forehead.

Wilda furtively gathered her tears on her
finger-tips, and hid them in her linsey dress,
but she said impressively to Alanson, —

" Now, that kiss will make you a better
man all your life."

SERENA

TIME, 1860

SERENA HEDDING drove through the gateway of her father's farm, while her little son
held the creaking gate open. Her vehicle
was a low buggy, with room at the back for
a sack of nubbins, which the scrawny white
horse would appreciate on his return trip.
The driver was obliged to cluck encouragement to him as he paused, with his head
down, in the gateway; and before he had
taken ten steps forward, before Milton could
stick the pin back in the post-hole and scam-
per to his seat at her left side, she lived her
girlhood over. She saw her father holding
that gate open for camp-meeting or pro-
tracted-meeting folks to drive in to dinner
with him. She saw Milton Hedding ride
through to court her, and the scowl her fa-

ther gave him; and the buggy which waited for her in the woods one afternoon, herself getting into it, and Milton whipping up his horse to carry her away forever.

The road wound, folding on itself, through dense woods. Nothing had changed about the road. She noticed that the old log among the haw saplings remained untouched. That log was a link binding her childhood to her girlhood. She sat on it to baste up the hem of her ridiculously long dress before going to school, her dinner-basket waiting near; and, coming home in the evening, she there ripped the basting out, lest Aunt Lindy should notice that her skirt did not flop against her heels, as proper skirts had done in Aunt Lindy's childhood. Seated on that log, she and Milton had talked of the impossibility of their marriage, and decided to run away.

It was so near sunset that the woods were in mellow twilight. She heard the cows lowing away off, and a loaded wagon rum-

bling over the Feeder bridge. The loamy
incense of this ancestral land was so sweet
that it pained her. Soon the house would
come in sight, and seem to strike her on the
face. If they had altered it any, she did
not know it. Was her father's sick-bed
downstairs, or did Aunt Lindy keep him
above the narrow staircase? The slippery-
elm tree she used to wound for its juicy
strips started out at the roadside to give her
a scarry welcome. Her fingers brushed her
cheeks, and drew the black sunbonnet farther over them.

" What's the matter, mother? " inquired
her light-haired boy. " Are you feared
grandfather's worse? "

" I hope he ain't," replied Serena. Then
the house, on its rising ground, appeared,
crossed by trees. It had a yard in which
lilac bushes and tall hollyhocks bordered
the path. The gate opened into an orchard,
and the orchard was guarded from the lane
by bars, which Serena's little boy let down,
and they drove in.

Her father's barn was one of those immense structures which early Ohio farmers built to indicate their wealth. It had always seemed bursting with hay and grain, and the stamp of horses resounded from its basement stables.

Serena looked piteously at the house. Vehicles of various kinds were fastened all along the fence. Still, no solemn voice or sound of singing reached her ear. It had long been the Jeffries custom to hold services over their dead at the house. No feather-bed hung across the garden palings; neither was the hideous cooling-board standing up anywhere, like a wooden tombstone. But the whole neighborhood was there. He must be very low indeed.

The youthful widow and her boy alighted, and tied their horse in a humble corner near the woodpile. Nobody came out to receive them. That was another bad sign. She was cramped by her long ride. If her suspense had not been so great she must have felt a pang of shame at the shabby appearance of her son and herself, on this first return from exile.

The house dog barked, waking suddenly from his meditations to learn who they were and what they wanted. But he recollected that a great many strangers had been coming and going recently, and considering his duty done, trotted back, and stretched himself to snap flies.

Serena felt obliged to go around to the front of the house, though the back doorstep showed the wear of her childish feet. But as she passed the first rosebush, Milty trotting in the white path behind her, a woman came from the back porch, holding a handkerchief over her cap, the ribbons of which flew back on each side of her neck. The light glared on her spectacles. She was as trim and quick as a young girl. Her dress, cape, and apron were of the same material, and her waist was fastened in front with a spiky row of pins.

" Serene Heddin' ! " she exclaimed, with
the spring in her voice which Serena remembered comparing to the clip of a mouse-trap,
" you 're not goin' into the front door to
scare your father to death in his last moments."

" Oh, Aunt Lindy," said the shabby
widow, lifting her hands, " is he as bad as
that ? "

" He 's been struck with death all the
afternoon.   You come in this way."

" Can't I see him ? " asked Mrs. Hedding, climbing over the back doorstone like
a suddenly exhausted pilgrim, her face quivering under streams of tears.

Through open doors she recognized in the
parlor and sitting-room groups of old neighbors, waiting in that hush with which they
always accompanied one another to the brink
of death.   A woman came from among
them, whispering, —

" Who 's this, Lindy ? " and immediately
informing herself : " Why, Sereny Jeffr's !

Have you got here ? Come right in to your
pap. He 's pretty nigh gone."

" It won't do no good, Sister McGafferty,"
said Aunt Lindy. " He won't know her,
and 't will disturb him. She was postin' in
at the front door when I caught her," declared Aunt Lindy, as if speaking of a thief.

Sister McGafferty, a comfortable, large
woman in blue spectacles, the presiding
elder's wife, and therefore a person of authority, still beckoned Serena in, and she
passed Aunt Lindy, followed by her barefooted boy. The round-posted bedstead was
drawn out from the wall, and under its sheet
and many colored quilt lay the old farmer,
his mouth open, his eyes glazed, his narrow
brows and knotty features wearing a ghastly
pallor. But behind the solemn terror of
that face was her father.

Aunt Lindy followed, and twitched her
elbow, thereby creating a faction in Serena
Hedding's favor among the spectators. They
were all well-to-do people, who noticed her

dejected attitude toward the world, and had always disapproved of her thriftless match. But they said within themselves that Lindy Miller was going too far when she tried to pull a daughter away from her dying father.

"Ain't you 'shamed to disturb his last peaceful minutes!" Aunt Lindy hissed with force.

But the returned culprit fastened such desperate interest on the unseeing eyes of her father that Aunt Lindy's interruption was as remote to her as the gambols of loose horses in the pasture.

If there had now been time and opportunity, Serena could not argue her case with him. He never had allowed that. She could not tell how true and happy her marriage was, in spite of his disapproval and its accompanying poverty. She had suffered, but her heart had ripened so that she could discern and love the good in human nature across its narrow bounds. Words or expressions did not occur to her; but a thousand living thoughts swarmed in her mind. If he would look at her again with reconciliation in his eyes, she could be satisfied, and bear all her future trials like benedictions. Never a loving father, he was, until her disobedience, a fairly kind one. He was a very religious man of the old sort, believing seriousness to be the primary principle of godliness, and levity a fermentation of the inward Satan. He always paid his quarterage and contributed to foreign missions, while every successive preacher on the circuit used his house as home. The deep grooves making a triangle of his upper lip showed how constant and sad his meditations had been. Yet this old farmer was in some matters timid and self-distrustful, and so fond of peace and quiet as to yield his rights for them.

" Father," pleaded Serena Hedding, bending closer to him. " Father ! " Unconsciously she repeated the name like a cry. The hum of the bee-hives against the garden

palings could be heard. Did a ray dart
across his leaden brain from the afternoon
his only child, in short coats, poked a stick
in the bee-hives, and, feeling the results of
her folly, wailed thus to him? Did he imagine himself again dropping the rake and
leaping the fence to run with her from her
tormentors? A flicker grew through the
glazing of his eyes, and became a steady
light, a look, a tender gaze, a blessing. She
clasped her hands, and rocked before him in
ecstasy. He knew her, and revealed, mid-
way over the silent chasm of death, how unalterably close and dear she was to him. In
that small eternity of time they were knitted
together as never before. His eyes began
to glaze again, and she remembered Milty.
Pushing the child forward, she cried again,
" My boy, father! See my boy! "

The old man saw him. That rigid face
was too set to smile, but with the image of his
child's child on his eyes, the hope of future
generations of his blood, he passed away.

A little time was allowed for the wailing
that rises around every death-bed. The
overtaxed young widow rocked her son
against her, while he gazed about him in
awe. Aunt Lindy stood by the bedpost,
burying her face in her apron. Her son,
Hod Miller, a huge creature, very black-
eyed, bright-complexioned, and having the
appearance of possessing no immortal soul,
sat near the foot of the bed, with his legs
crossed and his shoulders hung forward,
looking respectfully concerned. There were
no other near relatives except Jesse Jeffries
and his wife, who covered their faces while
this elder brother lay in the first dignity of
death.

Then a quiet bustle began. Sister Mc-
Gafferty took Serena Hedding out of the
parlor, and made her lie down on the sitting-room straw-tick lounge, and smell camphor. Milty wandered out-of-doors, and was
grateful to a neighbor's boy, forbidden the
house and enjoined to watch the horses, who

told him, after an exchange of scrutiny, that
he durs n't take a dare which 'ud reach the
medder fence first. The men took charge
of the body. They closed the parlor doors,
and, with basins of water, clean linen, and
the new store suit Aunt Lindy's forethought
had ready in the house, performed those
solemn rites to which all our flesh must
humbly come. One mounted a horse and
rode to Millersport for the undertaker. Little Jimmy Holmes, who was a middle-aged
man, but had a father known as Old or Big
Jimmy, was informed by his wife that he
could go home now, and look after the
milkin' and feedin'; she would stay here and
tend to things. Into her capable hands
Aunt Lindy appeared to resign the house,
while Little Jimmy and their son, Little
Jimmy's Jimmy, drove into the pleasant
dusk.

After inquiring about the date of the
funeral, and detailing watchers for the intervening nights, the other neighbors slowly

dispersed in squads. Lights appeared about the house, and the kitchen and cellar yielded up their prepared good things.

Before they reached home the neighbors began to speculate about the disposition of the property. They said Moses Jeffr's had been a hard worker, and his sister Lindy had been a hard worker, and she had kept his house for more than twenty year: 't would n't be no more than right for him to leave her well off. She had been savin' with what her man left her, and Hod Miller had done a son's part by the old man. Money goes to them that lays up. Some said Mr. Jeffr's had cut off Sereny with a cent in his will. Sereny ought to knowed better than to done as she did. It was a pity, specially as she was left a widow-woman, with a little boy to raise. But when a person makes their bed, they got to lie in it. How tickled Mr. Jeffr's was when Sereny was a little girl experiencin' religion! He never thought then she would go and run off. She had a good home, and he would have done well by her.

On the other hand, there was folks-talk among the Serena faction, whose hearts melted toward the girl when she rocked before her father. They said there never would have been any trouble between Moses Jeffr's and his daughter if Lindy Miller had n't managed things. Milt Heddin' was a good feller, only he had n't the knack of gettin' along. But he could have worked the farm as well as Hod Miller. They wanted Sereny to have her rights. It was a scandal and a shame if that big, able-bodied feller, with land of his own, could turn her off the home place.

Serena wandered about the house, which strangers seemed to possess, crying over familiar objects. She had large violet eyes, and was once considered as pretty a girl as came to meeting, though her lips were too prominent and full. She looked shabby and piteous. Sister McGafferty combed her hair

for her, while her trembling, work-worn
hands lay in her lap.

" They 've borried a black bonnet and
dress for you, Sister Sereny," said the
elder's wife, who had been around the circuit when this sorrowful creature was a shy
child.

" I might have worn a better dress and
bonnet. But when word came, I felt so bad
I did n't think of anything. They did n't let
me know until he was near gone."

Milty spent his time out-of-doors. He
approved of the barn, and did not approve
of Aunt Lindy. His mother had said,
" Aunt Lindy, this is my boy."

And Aunt Lindy had said, " He looks
spindlin', like the Heddin's. I hope you 're
raisin' him to obedience. Children set on
their own way gives their parents plenty of
sorrow to sup."

This spry great-aunt's glasses detected
him if he touched a daguerreotype among
the glaring, upright array on the sitting-

room table, or ventured too near the fine
men and women pasted on the fire-screen.

She took him to see his grandfather after
the laying-out, turned back the ghastly sheet,
which was stretched between two chairs, re-
moved cloths from the dead man's face, and
warned the boy to prepare for death. He
never afterwards inhaled the pungent odor
of camphor without turning faint.

At table he and his mother huddled together, feeling scarcely welcome to the abundant food. Little Jimmy Holmes's wife,
with a number of helpers, kept the table
burdened with every country luxury, but
Aunt Lindy saw that the best was reserved
until the great final dinner on the day of
the funeral.

That day was considered a credit to Moses
Jeffries. It was one of the largest funerals
ever known in those parts. The weather
was pleasant, and summer work so well ad-
vanced that everybody could feel the pres-
sure of neighborly duty. Carriages and fine

horses nearly filled the orchard space in front
of the house; the yard was darkened with
standing men in their best black clothes.
Not half the people could get into the house,
to say nothing of getting into the parlor.
There Elder McGafferty lifted his hands,
praying and preaching over the old farmer,
who looked so unused to his collar and neck-
cloth and brand-new suit when they took off
his coffin-lid.

A number of men wandered down by the
barn; the hymn-singing came to them faint
and plaintive, in gusts of couplets, just as
the preacher lined the words.

One of them remarked that old Mr.
Jeffr's left things in pretty good shape, and
he s'posed Hod Miller would n't alter them
much. Another thought that Serene Heddin' would come in for a sheer, if not all.
A man may be put out with his children,
but he 'll favor them when it comes to such
serious business as makin' a will. Hod
Miller had bought and sold and made money

on that farm, enough to pay for his work. He ought n't to stand in Sereny's light.

" What 's she been doin' since her man died ? " inquired the first speaker, shaving off long whittlings from a piece of pine.

" Workin' out, 'pears like I heard. She got a place near Lancaster, where they 'd let her keep her boy with her. It 's my opinion," said the second speaker, suddenly spitting a flood, and letting his spiky chin work up and down with slow rumination, " that old Lindy kept her away from her pap as long as she could, for fear there 'd be a makin' up."

" Oh, sho ! The old man was very set in his ways. He did n't need bully-raggin' to make up his mind and keep it made up. Hod Miller might marry the widder now, and that 'd settle all claims."

" I don't believe she 'd have him," said the chewer, smiling slowly. " Jesse Jeffr's, he thinks Sereny 's all right. He claims he seen the will."

The whittler scoffed at such claims. Jesse Jeffries was held in light esteem by his old neighbors. He sold his farm, and had such a hankering for town life as to settle in Millersport, the Deep Cut of the Ohio canal, and lose every cent of it in grocery-keeping. What Jesse Jeffries said or did thereafter was of small importance. His record slew him.

There was bustle at the front of the house. Both men squinted in the sun, and watched a long black object with shining dots upon it coming through the door, borne by stout young farmers. The men in the yard raised their hats. After the coffin came Serena, on her Uncle Jesse's arm. He shuffled along uncomfortably, as if not used to showing such attention to the women-folks. After them came Hod Miller and his mother, and Jesse Jeffries' wife with Serena's boy. Sister McGafferty considered this the proper order of procession, and had so managed it. Streams of people gushed from all the outlets of the house; the carriages filled and were arrayed in line; the long black serpent trailed down through the woods; and the women remaining to prepare dinner stood and counted, until they declared it beat everything. It was a pleasant sensation to be at such a populous funeral.

When Jesse Jeffries foretold the contents of the will he did not speak without authority, for it had been left in his hands. After a hearty dinner, at which many tablefuls of neighbors assisted, he importantly called the possible heirs together, and their factions sat by to listen.

Aunt Lindy was neither nervous nor bowed with grief. She had done her duty, and knew what her deserts were. Her son Hod tipped back in his chair, and twitched his shirt-collar. He wanted to have the thing over, and was not without doubts of his succeeding to the estate. If it came to him he meant to hold to it. His hands were as strong as a vise, and typified his grip on property. Serena might try to break the will, but if she lawed until Judgment Day he would not give her a cent he was not obliged to give her. Women-folks were a sort of cattle he had no fancy for.

Curious eyes watched Serena, and speculated on her emotions. She was pale and quiet. Her son stood beside her.

The testator's brother broke the seal, and began to read.

The testator, after stating his sanity and general ability to execute such a document, giving the numbers of his various lands and enumerating his parcels of property in the tedious and high-sounding repetition prescribed by law, bequeathed it all to his beloved daughter Serena Jeffries, and her heirs, the said Serena being enjoined to pay a stated annuity to her aunt, the testator's beloved sister, and to make over to her certain chattels particularly named; also a legacy of five hundred dollars to her cousin, Howard Miller.

Sister McGafferty poked the camphor bottle toward Serena, but it was declined.

Still the poor girl could not believe this. Disinheritance had been so long accepted as part of the penalty of her marriage that she scarcely thought of it as injustice. But to have the homestead for her own was a rise which made her dizzy.

After gazing on her with satisfaction through his glasses, Uncle Jesse turned the paper over, and rapidly read a small codicil, which nevertheless choked him. He knew nothing about this part of the will. It destroyed Serena Hedding's claims, on account of her disobedience, and made Howard Miller unconditional heir.

So that settled the matter. Serena turned whiter. It was a shock, after realizing one instant the possession of competence.

" I 'low Mozy must have put that on the day he took it away to have more added, he said," remarked Uncle Jesse huskily. His good wife, who was all cap-rim and beak, with a thin neck and general air of scrawn-iness, sat with her claws crossed in silent sympathy. Jesse and his wife did not find Lindy a congenial sister.

" Well," remarked Aunt Lindy, turning her head so the light fell in a sheet of glare upon her spectacles, " I 'm satisfied. That is, I will be when I 've said what I 'm goin' to say. I 'm a plain speaker, and tell my mind. Things has turned out right. Sereny Heddin' left her pap, and we stayed by him. She 's got her reward, and we 've got our'n. I hope you don't take no exceptions to his will, Sereny ? "

Sereny replied in a low voice that she did not take any.

" To show that I 'm fair-minded and want to do right by you," said Aunt Lindy, rais-ing her voice to the tone she used in speak-ing-meeting when exhorting sinners, " I 'll give you your mother's spinnin'-wheel that

stands in the smoke-house. You ought to
have something to remember her by."

Little Jimmy Holmes's wife nudged the
woman next to her, and whispered, with a
curving mouth, "Just the idy! And all
Sereny's mother's spoons, and her quilts
and coverlids she had wove! And the girl
never having any settin'-out in the first
place!"

Serena climbed the staircase, to take off
her borrowed mourning, and put on her own
shabby weeds for her ride back into the
world. She passed presses stacked with
household linen. The precious things of
her childhood, seen and handled in this trying visit, seemed so heart-breakingly precious
because Hod Miller's future wife would
throw them about as common. She would
like to have the yellow, leather-bound copy
of " Alonzo and Melissa," the novel of the
house, always considered unwholesome by
the elders, and as surely read with sly zest
by the children. The coverlet with her

mother's name woven into it had never been intended for anybody but the daughter of the house. It was unendurable to go away from home this second time, and into perpetual exile.

" Now I wisht they 'd find a later will," said Little Jimmy Holmes's wife, tying on her bonnet in the best bedroom. The persons who had lingered to support the family through the ordeal of will-reading were driving off, one after another. " Oh, but Aunt Lindy 'll carry things before her! Is she anywhere near? I don't want her to hear me."

" Things don't turn out that way except in novel-stories," observed another woman, with her mouth full of pins. " They don't find wills hid around in stockin's or Bibles. I declare, I 'm real sorry for Sereny. I don't see how old Mr. Jeffr's can lay easy in his grave, turnin' his own child out to give place to a big, hearty feller, with money in his own right."

"I always thought so much of Serene," said Little Jimmy Holmes's wife. "We was taken into full church membership on the same day ; and we used to run together and swap dinners at the Gum College. Aunt Lindy was so hard on her. I've asked Serene to go home with me and stay as long as she wanted to. But she has to take that horse and buggy back. And I don't think she could stand it, so near the old home."

"Now what do you think?" said Jesse Jeffries' wife, coming in, with her black-mitted hands pressed together. "Things is willed to Sereny, after all."

The bedroom resounded with ejaculations.

"How do you make that out?" inquired Little Jimmy Holmes's wife. "I'd give all my yearlin' calves to have it so."

"There was another piece wrote on to the paper, that Jesse missed. 'Pears like Mozy cut her off, and then repented, and went right to another lawyer and had it fixed, for it's in two different handwrites.

Things stands just as they did in the first."

" I 'm sorry Lindy gets her yearly portion," said Mrs. Holmes, in an irreverent aside. " Let me get out of this crowd : I 'm goin' to hug Serene."

" I *thought* 't was a great pity," exclaimed the woman with pins in her mouth, bestowing them rapidly about her bonnet ribbons, "if Sereny could n't have the homestead to bring up her boy in ! "

" You said folks never found new wills ! " observed a neighbor triumphantly.

" Well," retorted the woman, turning her face from side to side to get her chin set properly in the bonnet ribbons, " they *did n't* find any. Jesse Jeffr's only fooled around and did n't read all of the first one. They might 'a' knowed *Jesse Jeffr's* 'ud make a mess of it. *He* don't know how to do a thing right."

This opinion was shielded from the ear of Mrs. Jesse. She was busy nodding her leghorn bonnet and exchanging parting civilities with several old neighbors.

But Little Jimmy Holmes's wife had flown upstairs, and interfered with Jesse Jeffries and Sister McGafferty and a number of others. Serena lay upon a bed, and the air reeked with camphor.

"She's overcome like," explained Uncle Jesse.

"Let me get to her," said Mrs. Holmes. Having got to her, Mrs. Holmes raised Serena's head on her arm, and began to laugh.

"She's comin' out of it now," observed Sister McGafferty. "All of you'd better go downstairs except Sister Holmes and me. Let her be without disturbin' a while. We'll have plenty of other chances to enjoy Sister Heddin's company."

The neighbors and Jesse went submissively downstairs, but Little Jimmy Holmes's wife kept on laughing with some effort, as if she felt afraid of ending in a sob.

"Oh, I 'm so glad you 'll be in the neighborhood again, Serene!" she said. "Things would n't never been right in this world if they 'd turned out the other way. Don't look at me like you 's thinkin' of the dead. But rouse up and feel better. There 's your Aunt Lindy and Hod standin' at the gate : I can see 'em through the winder. They 're talkin' mighty serious, and she don't look so well satisfied as she did. But you must do well by her, Sereny. Give her the old spinnin'-wheel that stands in the smokehouse!"

ROSE DAY

"I DO believe this is rose day," said Infant, standing on the top step of the veranda in delight.

"I *know* it's soap-boiling day," asserted her twin sister, who had been baptized Marilla Victoria when she was baptized Infanta Isabella, quite forty years before. These twins entered the world at a period when flowery, daring names were the extreme of fashion, and previous to a rebound to plain and strong Ann, Elizabeth, Mary, Hannah, Jane, and their various combinations. Infant came very near being labeled Lovey Lucilla, and she felt thankful for her escape, and even attached to her diminutive.

Belle would never have suited her (she

was not belle), while Infant did not shame
her (she was more or less an infant at any
age). She was slender, blue-eyed, and
smooth-skinned, so smooth that wrinkles
could scarcely make their indentation. And
it never ceased to be appropriate for her to
wear her hair in a braid down her back,
tied with ribbons the color of the dress she
wore. Infant herself could not separate the
gray hair from the blond, nor did she care
whether it was all blond or all gray. She
scampered over a fence and swung in the
cherry-trees. Her long tranced girlhood
never ended; and the slow life of the farm,
simple as grass and wholesome as new milk,
kept up the illusion that time was eternity.
In their neighborhood these twins had been
the Baldwin girls when they first toddled
into meeting, when they went off to be
educated at an expensive school, when they
came back to paint and to play on a grand
piano, when their parents died and they
took charge of the farm; and the Baldwin

girls would probably be their title when they should become contemporary with all living grandmothers.

Occasionally Infant received a shock from the growth of young children. It was so astonishing to see a creature who was a baby but a short time ago, shooting aloft, long-armed and long - legged, and announcing itself in the teens. Such phenomena did not astonish Rilla, however. She resented them. Though she had the same fair complexion and comely make as her sister, a deadly drop of acid had been added to her nature. Her shoulders were bent. She loved to hear people talked about, and to lift the corners of her nose with scorn. She felt abused by much that had happened to her on this planet, and yet too insignificant in her own personality to take it out of the human race as she desired to do. The freedom, ease, and scope of mature unmarried womanhood were in no wise appreciated by her. These traits made Rilla an uncomfortable housemate, especially in winter, when the twins were snowed in with their books and trim housekeeping. Still, Infant loved Rilla's sourness along with Rilla. There was strong diversion in being scolded, and she always felt such a delicious warmth around her heart when she made it up with Rilla and gave her a handsome present, or took double turns at the cooking.

Rilla was very parsimonious, and felt bound to distort herself with aged gowns and long-hoarded hats. But Infant felt unhappy in any color except that tint of gray which has the thought of wine in it. On this very rose day, though it was early in the morning, she wore a clinging gray challie dress. And a good background it would be for all the roses Infant could hang upon it.

Nothing made Rilla lift the corners of her nose higher than Infant's flower days. But as Rilla would be lifting her nose anyhow, and could really scent no harm in these silent festivals, Infant continued to observe them year after year, and to afford her sister that triumphant sense of superiority which we all have upon beholding others' absurdities.

There was crocus day, when the first flowers broke the sod and made heavenly beauty in the dark spring. Infant decked herself with them, and put them on the dinner-table. More abundantly satisfactory, however, was lilac day. It took a critical eye to discern the exact date. If the lilacs browned about the edges, then, alas! lilac day had slipped past. They were not to be gathered too soon, either, if their full soul of fragrance was to be enjoyed. On lilac day Infant walked under burdens of lavender bloom. The walls, the pictures, breathed lilacs. And at night she went to sleep crushing her face into a nest of bunches, so that she had lilac dreams, and drew the sweetness into herself, like an Eastern woman absorbing roses.

But the best day of all was rose day. Be-

fore it arrived she had always ready a posy
of poems from Keats, Wordsworth, Jean In-
gelow, and Whittier, and read them in the
morning while the dew was on the world.
The Baldwin girls cultivated a great many
roses. Rilla could hardly miss from her
rose-water and home-made attar and rose
preserves the heaps which Infant cut for her
nonsense.

There was not a nicer day in the year
than rose day, if Rilla would only abstain
from boiling soap on that date. The sisters
had inherited seventy-five thousand dollars
apiece, but they made their own soap every
spring of refuse fats and the lye of wood-
ashes. It could have been made cold in the
cellar, if that way had not been too easy for
Rilla. She held it a movable festival, like
rose day, and no one will ever gauge the
degree of satisfaction she felt in haling her
flower-wreathed sister up to the vile-smelling
caldron to keep the stirrer going while she
set about other duties. Rilla honored pioneer

custom and her grandmother's memory by performing her soap incantations in the oldest, mouldiest, most completely shattered garment she possessed. This was a red wool delaine, so abased from its ruby tone that the drippings of the lye gourd could find little remaining space to burn or spot.

They boiled soap in a huge iron kettle in the chip yard. The blue wood smoke would envelop Rilla and her tarnished tatters as she ladled and tested, until she looked witch-like to passers along the road. Her unhappy victim, the slim woman in gray, with a rope of roses wound spirally around her from head to foot, a burden of roses on her bosom, and roses studded thickly along the band of her hat, sat on the corded wood as far as Rilla would allow from the soap, alternately inhaling their odor and rejecting the alkali steam. If Infant had to stir the soap, she would have a long-handled stirrer. The hot sun, beating on the chip yard and her huge hat, smote also the roses, and amidst their dying fragrance she had sad thoughts on the disappointments of life. So there was nothing but the morning of rose day which Rilla did not spoil.

But this anniversary Infant felt a sudden uplifting of courage within herself when her twin announced the soap orgy.

" *My* soap-boiling will not come any more on rose day," she put forth strongly. " And I think I will pay Enos Robb's wife to make up my share of the fat and lye after this, Rilla."

" I would," said Rilla sarcastically, " particularly as Enos Robb and his wife and children don't batten on us already. Give them the piano and the best parlor chairs and the solid coffee service while you are about it."

" Why, Rilla, I did n't propose to give her my share of the soap. But it would be cheaply got rid of that way. Yes," exclaimed Infant, with sudden recklessness, " I would rather *buy* soap, and pay out money to have this dirty stuff carted off, than ever smell it again while I live. Let us make a new rule, and give our fat and ashes to the Robbs. They have farmed for us ever since father died," Infant pleaded, " and whatever you say, Rilla, I know you have the greatest confidence in them."

" The poorhouse wagon is never going to call for me," said Rilla decidedly. " You can go and build a fire under the kettle, while I carry some more water to pour on the ash hopper. That lye is strong enough to bear up a setting of eggs, but we may need some more a little weaker."

" Rilla, I am as firm as the ash hopper itself. You can't shake me any more than you could our brick smoke-house. I won't help make any more soap — especially on rose day," added Infant to herself. " I don't see any sense in it."

" But you can see sense in spoiling dozens of good roses to load yourself up with like a mad Ophelia. You feel above all the asso-

ciations of wash day, though the Princess
Nausicaa did n't."

"Oh, Rilla, I don't feel above anything.
I merely feel under that soap kettle, and as
if it would crush my soul out, as the shields
crushed Tarpeia, if I did n't throw it off."

"Well, I am going to make soap," said
Rilla, whitening with intense disapproval of
the liberty her twin proposed to grasp.
"You are not a minor, and if you were, I 'm
not your guardian. But if you propose to
go to yourself and leave me to myself, we
both know what belongs to us, and it is
easily done."

This time-worn hint, which in her girlhood used to startle and distress Infant so
much, made but the slightest impression on
her hearing now, as she leaned over the
veranda railing to look at the roses. There
were such abundant stacks of them : she
might cut and pile them into a pyramid
almost as tall as herself. Such smooth,
sweet tea-roses, such crimson velvet-petaled

Jacqueminots, blush and white so fragrant
you would be willing to drown yourself in a
sea of their scent; yellow roses piercingly
delightful, Prairie Queens creeping all over
the front of the house, old hundred-leaved
varieties, having always in their depths a
reminder of grandmother's chests and long,
long past days. There were eighteen distinct families of roses, each family a mighty
tribe, marshaled before Infant on lawn and
dewy stretch of garden. It was rose day.
She would not let herself think of anything
else.

Rilla would not come to the embowered
dinner-table which Infant prepared so carefully, and to which she called her sister exactly as the clock struck twelve.

Rose day never interfered with Infant's
duties. Her conscience acquitted her of
shirking. Often in dead winter-time, when
the snow piled up, and Enos Robb's family
settled down to the enjoyment of colds and
rheumatism, she fed all the stock herself.

Rilla turned her back on Infant's several approaches, and dipped lye with a savagely noisy gourd to quench Infant's voice. Slugs and ants in the roses, and even mildew, were no drawback at all to rose day compared to Rilla. Habits of endurance become proof armor to one's sensibilities in the course of life, however; so Infant wandered off and absorbed the beauty of that day almost as completely as if she did so with Rilla's approval. There was tremulous heat over the meadows. The huge and strictly tended garden was a world by itself. Beyond that stretched their orchard, having a run of clear water winding through it, all thickly tufted along the margins with mint.

Infant stepped upon the spongy lichens of the fence and rested her arms on the top rail, while she looked along the narrow country thoroughfare. The sweet green world was dear enough to be pressed in her arms. Mingled mint and rose scents were satisfying. The noble strength of their Norman colts pasturing in the stock meadow was beautiful to the eye. Infant loved to hear the pounding of those tufted feet, and to note the brilliant blackness or gray dappling of the young creatures' coats glistening in the sun. She did not expect anything more unusual to happen on this rose day than her rebellion against Rilla and the splendor of the weather.

But who should come suddenly riding along the road, as if he had an appointment with Infant, and meant to keep it the moment she set her foot on the rail, but the Honorable Truman Condit, who many years before rode as instantaneously out of her sight! She knew him in a flash, although his hair showed gray around the ears, and much experience had added unspeakably to his personality. He was on a Condit horse, evidently riding around to look at his old neighborhood. There was a great tribe of the Condits, all well-to-do, high-headed people. The Honorable Truman had been the local bright young man of his generation. He went west, where, Infant heard, he became a Senator and did tremendous things.

She was suddenly conscious that her rose-studded braid was not wound up in a decent lump as she wore it before her class of young ladies in Sunday-school. She felt contemptible and out of her place in the human procession, although the Honorable Truman turned his horse straight into the fence corner to shake hands with her.

" Pretty nearly the same Infant Baldwin," he remarked. " But I do see some lines on your face."

" I suppose I've vegetated instead of lived all the time you have been doing so much," said Infant.

" Oh, I have n't been doing so much."

" We heard you had."

" We means Rilla and you. And you did n't marry ? "

" No," said Infant, feeling it a stinging indignity that he should mention it, after that courtship so long ago buried. *He* had married, and raised a family out west. Rilla was probably right when she said one woman was the same as another to a man.

" And how is Rilla? Is she as hard on you as she used to be ? "

" Oh, Rilla was never hard on *me*. She is quite well, thank .you. You 're coming up to the house to make us a call and take tea, are n't you ? "

" I thought I would."

Infant looked anxiously at the westering sun. She hoped Rilla would have the cold soap cut into cakes and boxed, and herself bathed, clothed, and in her right mind, before the Honorable Truman Condit rode up to their door.

"I want to have a talk with you first, though," he added. " And my way is to go right to the point. Why did you never marry ? "

" Come to that," retorted Infant, a spar-

kle breaking through her face, "why did
you marry?"

"In the first place, because you wouldn't
have me, and in the second place, because I
found a very good wife where I went. I've
been a widower now several years, and the
boys are settled. I'm loose from business
for almost the first time in my life, and back
here to look at the old neighborhood before
spending some years abroad. Your never
marrying has revived certain things. Maybe
you've forgotten."

Among her other thoughts, Infant was
conscious of recollecting how often she had
wished to go abroad if only some happy
friend could go along as a cushion betwixt
Rilla and her. She unfastened with a furtive
hand the rose rope wound about her, but,
unwilling to let so many precious roses go,
gathered it into loops on her arm.

"Did you ever know," pursued the Honorable Truman, "that Rilla told me you
were going to marry one of the Pierson
boys?"

" No ! " Infant cried out so suddenly that the horse started.

" She did," said the Honorable Truman.

" Why," stammered Infant, " how could you believe it ? "

" I was a hot-headed boy with more pride than sense. I would n't say anything to you about it."

" I remember your quarreling with the Piersons."

" Were n't you engaged to one of them ? "

" No; which one ? "

" Abner."

" I never was engaged to anybody except you," she retorted, burning hotly in the face, " and I did not admire that experience when you dropped me and went off. And I don't yet, though you do lay the blame on poor Rilla."

Plenty of time had Rilla for all the domestic countermarching she wished to perform before that conference by the fence ended. Unusually stirring were her tactics

too, for all the Robbs were haled up from
the tenant-house — Mrs. Robb to cook a
supper, and the young Robbs not actually
farming to run on errands.

It was six o'clock when Enos came riding
his plough-horses to the great barn. He
had turned off early on purpose to intercept
Miss Infant and find out what changes were
to be made. Infant hastened up the orchard, while the Honorable Truman hastened
to the same destination by the road. She
saw him leading his horse up the avenue,
and felt impatient at Enos Robb's interruption.

"Sudden doin's up to the house," said
Enos, wiping his forehead with the back of
his hand. "'Pears like Miss Rill's made
up her mind about Brother Sanderson at
last."

"Is Brother Sanderson at the house?"
inquired Infant.

"He is, for a fact, and the license and
the preacher with him. Now what I want

to know, and what I ought to been con-
sulted, Miss Infant, seeing how long I been
here, is this — what's you and me going to
do afterward? Is it an interference?"

"Enos," said Infant, with a gasp, "this
is *almost* as sudden to me as it is to you.
But considering Rilla's firm character, do
you think she would let any new person
interfere with her established plans?"

"No, I don't," replied Enos, grinning.

Rilla was standing before the dresser in
her room arrayed in her stiffest silk. She
looked with composure upon her twin, who
shut the bedroom door, and hurried up to
embrace her.

"It was the best boiling of soap I ever
had," said Rilla, warding the fading roses
away from her silk.

"Rilla dear, you might have told me
what you meant to do this evening. But
I am so glad! I could n't bear the thoughts
of leaving you before, but now I can."

"I saw Truman Condit come into the

yard with you," said Rilla. "He's grown fat. It must have agreed with him to go west."

"This has been a great rose day," said her twin, undoing all traces of the day's festival, and piling them carefully in a waste-basket where they could make no litter. "Won't you let me kiss you, Rilla?"

The acquiescent nip which Rilla gave Infant took up a world of forgiveness which Rilla never felt.

"And do you think, dear," Infant ventured, "we'll ever wish we hadn't? We've lived so long with each other. Truman Condit and Brother Sanderson are really strangers to our ways."

"I think," replied Rilla, with decision, "that Brother Sanderson will never have a rose day while he lives on *my* farm; and when I say it is soap-boiling day it will *be* soap-boiling day, and Brother Sanderson will stir the soap."

KENTUCKY

A KENTUCKY PRINCESS

TIME, 1857

THE perfection of summer noon, when acres of corn tassels seemed in a trance and the blueness of far-off hills suggested incense rising, was not without its effect on Miss Sally Vandewater as she rode toward General Poynton's plantation. The turnpike, stretching its ash-colored ribbon across the greenness of the country, rang like a causeway of rock to the beat of horseshoes.

From this plantation or from that, as hill or sweep of woodland revealed them, shone marble stones in family burial lots.

Occasionally Miss Sally met girls or young men on dashing horses, and these merry people saluted her cordially in passing. But in all that blue-grass region, where each member of every comfortable family had his

own gaited saddle-horse, there was not a
finer animal than Miss Sally's Pacer. Cæ-
sar and his fortune were aboard when she
mounted. Pacer was her entire capital in
life, carrying her on visits among good families whereby she subsisted, and furnishing
colts for her pin-money. The camel is not
more to the Bedouin. Had Pacer failed
Miss Sally in any point, she must have fallen
into the straits of a reduced gentlewoman,
instead of carrying a high head through all
the best houses of the county.

She rode at a steady hand gallop through
the sultry day, though a young colt whinnied
behind her; increasing her speed past one
pillared brick house set far up an avenue.
The woods about it were close trimmed and
free from underbrush, like all Kentucky
woodland. Some evergreens made gloom
about its eaves, but not such gloom as the
reputation of the house itself. There lived a
man who was said to have a chain stretched
across his cellar. He bought up slaves and

handcuffed them in pairs along this chain until he was ready to drive them to market, when a band of musicians was employed to lead their march, cheerfully playing " Yankee Doodle." The house was worse than haunted. Both whites and blacks hurried past its handsome gate with abhorrence — spot of mystery and abomination on those pleasant corn lands.

Miss Sally was anxious to get out of her riding-skirt at Poynton's, and bully the black boy who would come to take her bridle. The wealthiest slave-owner in Kentucky could not exact more deference. Everybody humored her. In a country where hospitality was a social religion, her little visits of a month or two were welcomed even when they crowded dearer guests. And in spite of fine traits concealed under the haughty airs of a nomad, well did she know how to crowd people distasteful to her.

When she turned into Poynton's avenue, the white pillared mansion seemed to doze.

The quarters stretched in a long row field-
ward. Miss Sally could not see the kitchen,
standing by itself behind the great house.
No drowsiness had settled there. A stir of
preparation was going on, not only for the
two o'clock dinner, but for the wedding yet
a week distant. Miss Sally had omitted one
place in her rounds, and shortened her visit
at another, that she might be at Poynton's
in time to gather every detail of the wedding.

A yellow boy skipped out to help her at
the mounting-block. He would have lounged
to meet his master. Approvingly she saw
him pull his hat to her.

"Miss Sally, you sho'ly bake you'se'f to-
day!"

"Yes, it's hot, Peach. And if you're
concerned for me I hope you'll feel more
concern about Pacer." Miss Vandewater's
anxiety about her property grew in the ratio
of its approach to a crib.

"Sam'll rub her down," promised Peachy.
"I'll tell Sam to give her a good feed."

" You attend to it yourself," commanded Miss Sally.

" I is n't a stable - boy," remonstrated Peachy. " I 'se a house-boy."

" House-boy or stable-boy, you mind what I tell you. In my father's time — and he owned fifty — our boys did whatever they were told to do."

" Ya-as, m'm."

" And the poor little colt," said Miss Sally, making that infant's discomfort her own, — " I don't want my colt kicked to death among a lot of wild shod heels."

" He go with his mammy. No ha'um evah happen to you' colts on this place, Miss Sally."

" You see to it that none happens to it this time ! All the family at home ? " she stopped to inquire, with her riding-skirt gathered in her hand.

" Ya-as, m'm."

" Has my trunk been carried up ? I sent it this morning."

" Ya-as, m'm."

" Who 's here ? " demanded Miss Vandewater, stiffening her figure.

Peachy followed her eye to the stable-
yard, where stood a vehicle she never beheld
with calmness. It was the handsome and
shining carriage of Judge Poynton, from
the county seat.

Peachy grinned. " Miss Judge come out
this mawnin' to spend the day."

So sore does one's pride become when
chafed by poverty, that Miss Sally hated that
plump and opulent woman for naught but
being plump and opulent; though she would
have given as her reason the airs of a woman
married above her wildest expectations.

" You can fetch my riding-skirt to my
room, Nancy," said Miss Sally to the colored
girl who admitted her, casting it across the
stair-rail as she ascended. " I reckon I go
to the same room I always have."

" Miss Ma'ky's things is all spread out in
that bedroom," apologized Nancy.

" You can soon move them out of the way."

" But Miss Maria 'bleeged to have you' trunk set in the back bedroom fo' this week, Miss Sally."

A solicitous hostess, trailing a muslin wrapper — for even Kentucky hospitality may be overpowered by the languors of summer midday — met the guest with outstretched hands. Miss Sally permitted her cheek to be brushed, and at once put the lady into the apologetic attitude of an overcrowded landlord.

" You ought to have sent me word if it was inconvenient to have me now, Mrs. Poynton, and I would n't have skipped the Moores as I did."

" Miss Sally, it is not inconvenient to have you now ! " the delinquent pleaded. " It is never inconvenient. Only America's things are so spread out, and we are obliged to keep dressing-rooms for the wedding, and the bridesmaids ! I thought you would be

less annoyed in that back room than anywhere else. I am so glad you have come!"

"The judge's wife is here?"

"But it is only for the day," unconsciously
conciliated Mrs. Poynton. "She is not
staying. Sue Bet Moore has been here,
helping America to try on. Her dresses are
all done. But Sue Bet has gone."

"I knew Sue Bet was to be one of the
bridesmaids," said Miss Sally. It was not
necessary to mention bridesmaids to a woman of her thorough information.

"We have all been lying down; the day
is so sultry. We shall not have America's
things filling up the chambers much longer.
I feel like giving her all the rooms in the
house — yes, the plantation itself! If you
can only make yourself comfortable a few
days, we can change your room after the
wedding."

"The back bedroom makes not the slightest difference in the world to me, Mrs.
Poynton" —

" O Miss Sally, I am so glad it makes no difference ! "

— " but I am sorry I came at such an inconvenient time ! "

Thus the duet went on, until Mrs. Poynton accepted as positive beneficence Miss Sally Vandewater's willingness to descend from the back chamber, dine with the family, and sit down in the parlor.

Miss Sally had kept her sprightliness and her youthful shape. Her muslin dress was cut low, and her shoulders were concealed by a bertha of lace. Fine embroidered undersleeves made delicate frills about her folded hands. The curling-iron had created two large spirals at each temple, but the rest of her hair was pinned in a knot at the back of her head.

America Poynton came into the parlor in her tight-fitting habit of black velvet, and sat down with the guests, holding her riding-whip, her gauntlets, and tall hat.

" Are you going to ride in this heat ? " inquired her aunt, the judge's wife.

" We always ride Thursday afternoons, about four o'clock, if the weather is fine," America replied.

She looked no less cool and white in the heavy fabric than in a gold dotted vaporous tissue which she had worn at dinner. Her black eyes moved with languid interest from speaker to speaker as the visiting chat ran on. America Poynton was called the proudest girl who ever appeared in the county seat from surrounding plantations. The manners of this tall beauty were considered too quiet by romping young people who danced, drove, and flirted to the limit of their privileges; yet she was sovereign among them, and ruled by a look while others expended noisy effort. It was told of her that she often sat veiled in her room to save her complexion from sun glare and wind, so matchless was it. She had a robe of black curls in which she could wrap herself when her maid let it down to brush. America was General Poynton's only child.

She had inherited from her grandmother a plantation adjoining her father's, with more than a hundred slaves. When she went to boarding-school in the county town, one of her servants led to her every pleasant Friday evening a milk-white mule, saddled and bridled with silk, fine leather, and silver.

Though above such pastime as flirtation, America had more offers than any other girl in her set. Her low, slow voice never recounted these conquests, but the victims published themselves, wondering whom America Poynton would marry, since she was so hard to suit. When she accepted Ross Carr, therefore, the astonishment was general. He was good enough for some girls, but hardly good enough for America Poynton. He had also been a wild youth, but people said he was settling down. The Carrs ranked somewhat below the Poyntons, and Ross had no plantation of his own. Yet when the community thought it over, they were willing to accept him as America's husband if he proved a credit to her.

" Miss Maria," said Nancy, coming to the door with a face full of meaning, " Miss Becky Inchbald's done lighted down by the quarters, and tied her horse."

" What does she want ? " inquired Mrs. Poynton, disturbed.

" Dunno, Miss Maria."

" Why does n't she come to the house ? "

" She hardly ever came to the house in her best days," murmured the judge's wife.

" Perhaps she's sick," continued Mrs. Poynton. " Some of you run and see."

" Peachy done been down to her, and she say she just waitin' there in the shade. Miss Becky got her baby 'long with her."

The general's wife heard this with rising dignity.

" Don't annoy her," she commanded. " Let the poor girl alone."

" Law, Miss Maria, nobody won't say

nothin' to Miss Becky. But all the little niggehs has come out to look at her."

" Go yourself and see if she needs anything."

" I have heard," remarked Miss Vandewater, through the silence which followed, " that Becky Inchbald, for all she was so close-mouthed at first, threatens now to carry her child to its father."

Mrs. Poynton, with an instant's pause on the subject, hoped he could be found and made to do his duty. The judge's wife heard with a mere lifting of the eyebrows. She thought it scarcely a fit topic to mention before America. But America's plane was so much above Becky Inchbald that she had never even disapproved of the girl.

Becky Inchbald's people were not poor whites, for they owned land and slaves ; but their raw unfitness for encountering the old stock held them on the verge of society. That Becky was uneducated was her own fault. She had become the mother of a hapless baby and the scandal of the neighborhood before America Poynton's engagement was announced.

" She 's spiteful about that baby," pursued Miss Sally. " There 'll be trouble somewhere before sundown, if she 's started out with it."

" I do not see that Inchbald's affairs need disturb us," suggested the judge's wife, making dimples at the finger roots of one hand as she smoothed her polished hair.

" Some women are never disturbed about any of the sin in the world," said Miss Vandewater incisively, " until it comes into their houses and takes their children by the throat."

"That can never be said of you, Miss Sally," the judge's indolent wife responded, smiling. Though she generally bore Miss Sally's attacks as a lady should, and felt indulgent sympathy for the migratory spinster, she sometimes allowed herself to retort.

"Aunt and Miss Sally, kiss and make up," said America, with the deliberate accent that gave weight to all her words. But without response one of the combatants sat glowering, while the other, waving a lazy fan, indicated through the window Ross Carr cantering to his appointment, man and steed moving like one, so perfect was his horsemanship.

America's mother, impatiently anxious to go on recounting to Miss Sally the silver and linen bought for America's new home, resigned herself for a few moments. Ross Carr threw his bridle to the groom, who was walking Miss Poynton's saddled thoroughbred.

He entered the room. America gave him her hand with a light word, and he stood holding his hat, talking to her elders.

It was the culminating moment of her betrothal, a dot of time separating ease and care-free thoughts from what followed.

The young man chatted idly with four

women, when another screamed out behind
him : —

" Here it is, Ross Carr ! So you 've got
to take it, and no words betwixt us — for I
won't take care of it any longer ! "

" Why, Miss Becky !—why, Miss Becky ! "
Mrs. Poynton herself ran gasping forward
to interpose between such scandalous outcry
and America's lover. " Come away with me,
Miss Becky, and let me help you with your
baby — and don't speak that way before
the gentlemen ! "

A shaker bonnet fell back from the girl's
hot and furious face. She had narrow
sunken temples like a hen's. Her entire
profile was chicken beaked, yet a fluff of
golden down made her comely. The wrathful rings in her eyes sent out their fires
toward Ross Carr.

" He thinks he 's a great gentleman, and
he thinks he 's going to get a great lady " —

" Becky Inchbald, sit down in that chair ! "
commanded America, standing at the other

side of the room. Her hat and gloves and whip lay on the floor. The other women, even her mother, waited, sitting blanched.

Carr remained with his hand on the back of the chair, like a frozen figure, while Becky Inchbald placed herself in it and stretched the baby across her lap. Her first courage leaving her, she began to cry.

The men of the west do not cower when found out in their sins. Ross Carr stood six feet and one inch high; a handsome, light-haired Kentuckian, the man most abundant in vitality, and the best horseman in Bourbon County. A culprit waiting to be shot, he looked his death in the face, erect, but blighted through every outline. He had carried this guilt a long time, trying to shape it for disclosure; while day after day continued to separate him farther from the Ross Carr of the past, and to make more incomprehensible the deeds which he inherited from that miserable wretch.

When you or I stand, on our day of judgment, to be looked at through the dark medium of our basest moments, may some eye among our contemners discern the angel shape struggling in remorse and anguish behind the bar.

" Is this your child ? " America demanded of her lover, pointing to it for his identification.

The baby, oppressed by the jaunt, under arm, or on lap, according to its mother's convenience in riding, was covered all over its visible surface by that prickly rash which nurses call " heat." It was gowned in pink calico, and diffused a sour odor.

Ross Carr looked down at it with the slighting masculine eye, which since Saturn has seen little to admire in extremely young offspring. He controlled the muscles of his lips to reply.

" I reckon it is."

" Answer me on your word as a man — is this your child ? "

" Yes. It is."

" He knows it 's his, and he 's got to take care of it and support it — it 's his place to take care of it, not mine," sobbed Becky, her head wagging.

America directed her face to Becky. " Do you intend to turn it off entirely ? "

" Yes. I do! It 's his, and he ought to keep it! "

" But you are its mother! "

" I won't be its mother ! " exploded Becky, flinging the ill-kept and wretched infant about on her knees with a vicious grip. " I 'll leave it on a doorstep first! "

The child put up a piteous lip and uttered those cries by which bruised infancy protests against tormentors whom it feels but does not know.

America stared at the girl ; her alabaster face was suddenly drained of horror at the wrong done a woman, and filled with passionate contempt.

" Then I 'll be its mother! Give it to me."

She gathered it off Becky's lap and laid its heat-blotched face against her shoulder. The tiny creature discharged a mouthful of its wretchedness there. America stanched the spot, and made a softer rest for its cheek with her rose-scented handkerchief. Her unconscious sweep of figure in taking the child and standing up publicly with it, thrilled beholders like piercing music or the sight of great works of art. The mother-spirit, which has brooded for centuries over this world — the passion to foster and protect and train — shone white and large in her face. She was that fair impersonation men call the Goddess of Liberty, holding the outcast to her breast. She was Mother Mary, with a reminder of the Heavenly Infant in her arms.

No one remonstrated or spoke a word to her as she moved from the room.

Becky Inchbald, pulling her shaker over her face, went out and mounted her horse.

America was at the top of the stairs when

she heard Ross Carr speak hoarsely at the foot. She stood looking at him over the balustrade. The baby was quiet.

" One word, America! — It's all over — between us ? "

He could hear his watch ticking; and outdoor sounds buzzed in his ears.

" No," answered America. " It is not all over between us."

Ross Carr dropped his groping hand on the stair newel, his next sentence also coming in fragments.

" There won't be any use — Shall I come here — for the ceremony — next Thursday ? "

" Thursday," spoke the low, slow voice above him, " at two o'clock, was the time we set."

The culprit lifted his eyes to her and exclaimed : —

" America, tell me what you want me to do ! "

" I want you," she said, " to be a father

to your child!" Her mouth struggled. She flung out the rest in a wail — "and never speak to me of this again!"

Not fit to prostrate himself before her virgin motherhood, the tarnished man hid his face on his arm against the stair-rail. She carried his child out of sight.

There was scarcely a negro on the plantation who did not know what had happened when Ross Carr staggered out of the house and passed his chafing horse and the groom as if he had forgotten his own property.

Baseless mountains which had been piling lucent peak over peak, now seemed to sink in smoke to the effacement of the sun. Stretches of forest and road, plantation and dimpled hill, from horizon to horizon, ceased smiling; for the day's heat was about to pass off in drenching rain.

This cloudy interval before the thunderburst was just the time for stealing corn to roast at the quarters in the evening. So Peachy crept on all fours down narrow avenues to avoid agitating the corntops, such telltales are the tassel fingers. His sack already bulged ; but unexpectedly he came against a man stretched out in the dirt face downward — Miss Ma'ky's Mist' Ross Carr !

Peachy backed away from the spectacle, the grinding of teeth and the swelling of veins on a man's neck ! Not until many cornstalks screened him had Peachy the courage to burst recklessly down a slim alley, spilling his stolen ears, while corn leaves slashed his face with their edged sabres. The superstitious African instinctively fled from anguish so dumb and dreadful.

While the county was shocked by America Poynton's adoption of Ross Carr's child, her beauty as a bride softened all critics. She went to live with her husband on her plantation, and there the baby grew into robust and happy boyhood. Reticence on the subject of Becky Inchbald was diffused through her small world. At that date a

small world held all the acts of many
lives.

Even Miss Sally Vandewater, swelling
her visiting list with another hospitable home,
grew into complete harmony with the judge's
wife on this delicate subject.

Becky Inchbald went on a long visit to .
Tennessee. News came back that she had
married there; and in the course of years
that she had died.

So far as human knowledge goes, Ross
Carr's wife took no shrewish revenge,
though a woman of her nature must have
suffered from the blot. She always spoke
of his son as " our eldest boy," and he grew
up among brothers and sisters without noting
that he was part alien, until some neighbor
dropped the fact in his ear. Personally he
was much like his father, whose sin matured
its bitterest fruit when that child threw himself on the ground to sob in secret agony
because the beautiful and tender woman he
loved with such devotion was really not his
mother.

INDIANA

THE FAIRFIELD POET

Time, 1881

Tragedy, which is never far from the
most prosperous lives, continually trod upon
the tenderest-hearted woman in Fairfield.
She hated Fairfield as a background to her
existence, but there had fate nailed her for
life. It was the forlornest of Indiana railroad stations, looking like a scar on the face
of a beautifully wooded country, peopled by
the descendants of poor white Carolinians
and Tennesseeans. The male portion of the
community sat on the railroad platform in
yellow jeans, sprawling their naked toes to
the sun, whittling, and jetting with the reg-
ularity of fountains upon the meerschaum-
colored boards. The women might have
lived lives of primitive simplicity, dignified
by child-bearing and neighborly sympathy

with one another ; but they stained their
human kindness with trivial disagreements.

This one among them all felt the progress
of the age tearing her heartstrings out while
her circumstances kept her at a standstill.
I do not say her life would have been more
symmetrical or her experience richer if she
had lived in the whirl. She was a plain,
ground-loving woman who enjoyed the companionship of her fruit-trees and flowers, and
worked with her hands. Indeed, crowds
annoyed her, and she was undecided what
toilets ought to be made for a large public.
The striped silk dresses of her prosperous
days, the fringed crape shawls and gimp-
edged mantillas, agreed ill with bonnets of
the passing season, and she had more respect
for what was rich and old than for new inventions. But she was fiercely ambitious
for her children, especially her eldest son,
and for him in spite of his misfortune.
The younger boy and girl were still leaping
like colts upon their few remaining acres,

sound in limb and wind, with the hopes of a future sheathed in their healthy present, when Willie was tall as a man, and far up in his teens.

His mother had a picture of him taken when he was going to school in Cincinnati, under his uncle's care. At that time his auburn curls were unshorn, and he was beautiful.

A few days before cottons took their terrific rise during the civil war, Mr. Harbison had stocked in thousands of yards. Those were Fairfield's best days, and he kept a general store, making money so rapidly that the lazy people around him felt helplessly injured. He began his fine brick house, building on a generous and artistic plan, at the edge of Fairfield, where he could surround himself with fruit - trees, and have fields for his cattle. Whether it is a more distinct misery to build the temple of your home and see some one else inhabit it, or to shelter yourself for years in a house you have not the power of finishing, the latter fate was reserved for the Harbisons. With a crash they came down from what had been Fairfield's opulence nearly to a level with Fairfield's poverty. They kept the house and grounds and a meadow, but under such weight of mortgages that it was comparatively no grief at all to see the ornamental cornices lying around the partly plastered parlors, balustrades and newel-post standing on end beside the skeleton stairway, and to find the bathroom useless except as a rubbish closet. The man who had employed half of Fairfield was now obliged to become himself an employee, and the general verdict of the world against those who fail was emphasized by communistic envy.

But the habit of being a woman of consideration is not easily forgotten. Mrs. Harbison still made the village respect her. She had something to give to the poorest. She was the wife of a man who had made a fortune before he lost it, and sat in the state Senate.

More than all, she had her children, the eldest of them a continual surprise to her. He
seemed born to stir her pride and tender-
ness to their depths. He was tall, fair, and
Roman-featured, shy as a girl toward every
one but his mother, and so ravenous in
mind that he was partly through college
when his father's reverses brought him
home.

Then he was seized with a spotted fever,
and approached the next world so close that
he left part of his faculties there, and was
never the same Willie he had been before.
He could hear nothing, and seldom spoke an
audible word — Mrs. Harbison's boy, who
was made to take the world by storm — and
what had been the shyness of a country-bred
youth became the set-apart seclusion of a
hoofed and goat-eared faun. Willie Harbison was to be seen whirring as noiseless as a
bat upon his bicycle across the open ground
at dusk. He was met coming from the
woods, silent as an Indian, and his eyes were

on everything in earth or sky except the human beings just before him.

Whatever were the faults of Fairfield, it loved and respected Willie Harbison, and humored his self-withdrawal. And he loved Fairfield with a partiality which saw mere picturesqueness in the row of whittling men, and various forms of motherhood or sister-hood in the women. He would dismount from his wheel to let the boys tilt with it at the old warehouse. He loved the woods; he loved Wild-cat and Kitten creeks, which ploughed rock-bedded channels through the woods; and what joy in life he fished out of those waters only Willie himself knew. He loved to watch from the mill, on a clear morning, that plume of steam the south-bound train sent around the curve, to watch another plume roll over the first, and finally to see the train stand suddenly on the summit of the grade, sharp-cut against the sky. All com-mon life was pleasant to him. Who but his mother could be witness that a double nature dwelt under his floury mill clothes?

Willie worked in the mill with his father, where the roar of grinding and bolting and the whir of belts made silent liveliness around him. This had been bitterness to his mother — her Willie should work with his head alone; but she accepted it as the result of his physical misfortune.

The parlors were Willie's workshop, in which he sawed, hammered, and glued, or put noiseless inventions together. A carpenter's bench was set before two uncased windows, and his father's old store desk had fallen to his unmercantile use. Its lock was never opened unless Willie had something which he could force himself to show to his mother. That ripe instant arriving, he sought her in her kitchen, her garden, or at her spinning-wheel upstairs, and seized her by the hand. She went with him to the parlors, they fastened the doors, Willie undid his desk, and placed his paper in her fingers. The paper itself was sometimes brown, sometimes the blue cap left from the store, sometimes gilt-edged note having penciled landscapes along the margins, or the flowers he rhymed of done in water-colors; for his hand was as skillful as his eye was discerning. The poems were usually short, and sensitive in rhyme and rhythm. Willie's themes were the common sights and the common pathos or humor of the situations in which he found the people around him: his interpretation of the flicker's feelings; his delight in certain thick fleeces of grass; the panorama of sky and field as it marched across his eye; the grotesque though heartily human family party made by old man Persons and his wife, where half of their descendants, unable to get into the small house, sat on the fence while the rest ate dinner. Willie was deaf, but he had inward music. Every smooth and liquid stanza was like wine to his mother. She compared his poems to Burns's, and could not find the " Mountain Daisy " a whit better than her poet's song about the woods in frost.

Even Mr. Harbison thought well of Willie's performances. They were smuggled to him by the mother, and carefully returned to their place when the poet was out of the house. Mr. Harbison knew all that was going on in the world. A dozen times a year he left the grinding of the mill to meet his old chums at the capital, or to quicken the action of his blood in Chicago. A couple of stimulating days tinctured and made endurable his month of mill work. A man of luxurious tastes cannot lose his tastes with his means. He was a judge of poets, and said Willie might as well take to poetry as to anything, for business did not pay a man of sound faculties in these days.

The hum of bees could be heard all around this unfinished brick house growing mossy at the gables, and its shadow was long on the afternoon sunshine. It was that alert and happy time of year when the earth's sap starts new from winter distillation.

You could hear the voices of children calling in play as they loitered home from school; the days were so long that the cows would not come up the pasture until nearly seven o'clock.

Willie trudged across lots to supper. Mrs. Harbison met him at the north side of the house, having her garden knife and rake in her hands. She put them on the step-less front-door sill, which had never been and never would be pressed by the foot of an arriving guest. This stone sill was high enough for a seat, and she sat down, tilting her sunbonnet back, and smiling at Willie. He was floured from head to foot. Little of his boyish beauty except its clear innocence remained to him. His nose was large for his head, and on his head the auburn curls were shorn to a thin crisping layer.

His young sister was putting supper on the table in the dining-room, his brother was fisting with another boy on the railroad, and up the cow lane came his father with the slow step and somewhat of the ponderous white presence of the walking statue in " Don Giovanni." But closest knit of all this family, mother and son talked together in silence, some birds in the mulberry-tree over their heads making the only calling and replying that could be heard. Before Willie reached her, he held up his hands and signed in the deaf-mute language : —

"The preacher has come back."

Mrs. Harbison raised her hands and darted her fingers into various shapes, saying thereby, " Did you see him ? "

" No," Willie replied as swiftly ; " I only saw his coffin in the wagon, and Nancy Ellen sitting beside it. She had to bring him the whole twenty miles from where he died, in a wagon."

" Because it was n't on a railroad ? "

Willie nodded.

His mother wove on : " Poor Nancy Ellen ! Her father would n't let her have the preacher for so long, and turned her off when she did marry him. Now she's a widow in her honeymoon, and old man Morton saying he told her a preacher as old as himself was n't any match for her. Did you see her father? How did he act?"

" He got into the wagon by the driver," said Willie's fingers.

" Well, that was something for him."

" And they drove to his place."

" I suppose he 'll let her come back and live at home now."

" I wish you had seen Nancy Ellen."

" I 'm going to see her after the milking is done."

" Seen her by the preacher," insisted Willie's passes. " She looked like a captive coming in chains to Rome."

" Yes, I 'll be bound she did. Every jolt of that twenty miles is stamped in *her* mind."

" I wish," flashed Willie, " I knew what the preacher sung to himself all along the road."

"What a notion! You 'll have to fix it up in poetry now, won't you ? "

Willie shook his head many times and reddened.

"You said the preacher used to sing home from meeting in the dark."

" Yes, he did," affirmed Mrs. Harbison. " And Nancy Ellen used to listen for him to go by their place."

Their talk paused, and Willie looked up at the birds in the mulberry. Having afterward caught his mother's eye, he wove out slowly : —

> " When in the tree above his head
>> The sap goes tingling through the bark,
>> She will remember it was dead,
>> And hear him singing in the dark."

" Oh, Willie, is that the first verse or the last? Have you written it down ? "

Willie smiled shyly, putting his head down toward one shoulder, without making any reply. His mother urged, with eager fingers : —

" Print it in some place when you get it done.   Nancy Ellen would be pleased."

" I 'm not an obituary poet," wove Willie.

" But that 's so good."   Mrs. Harbison moved her lips, repeating it to herself. " And ain't you ever going to publish anything you write ?   I 've heard of people getting money for it."

Willie uttered a gentle sneer.   He laughed at his mother in a way that always made her laugh with him.

" But if you would let your father fix up your writings," she continued, repeating an old plea, " and send them to some publishing house, I know they would put them in a book for you."

The gate, weighted by a stone, slammed to behind his father coming to the evening meal.   But before his mother rose, Willie found time to make dance before her eyes the characters indicating this promise : —

" Some day I 'll get on my bicycle and ride and ride until I come to a publisher.

If you miss me, you'll know where I've gone. You can just say to yourself, ' He's off having his poems published.' Wait till then, mother; that will be soon enough."

" You'll never do it," said his mother, having no idea how near the time was.

She gave her family their supper and helped to milk the cows. She thought of Willie's stanza when the milk first sang in the pail, and kept repeating it until the rising froth drowned all sounds of the lashing streams quite at her pail's brim.

When the house was tidy and full of twilight stillness, Mrs. Harbison put on a clean apron and took her sunbonnet to make her call of condolence. It was likely they would want watchers at Morton's, and she was ready to do anything. She had helped bear the burden of life and death so long in Fairfield that illness, a new baby, or the mysterious breathless presence in any house was a peremptory invitation to her.

The boys were playing hide-and-seek

around the warehouse, and as she crossed the open lot she saw the usual line of wise men sitting on the edge of the platform with their legs across the rail, as if they had all agreed to make an offering of their feet to the Juggernaut of the next passing train.

Willie darted like a bat or a night bird on his bicycle far up and far down the smooth wagon road. Now he took a turn, and came spinning among the boys, scattering them before him, and escaping as often as they chased him. In one of these excursions he crossed his mother's way.

The last red streaks and high sunset lights were not gone out of the sky. She lifted up her hands and spelled, " Are you starting out to hunt a publisher now ? "

And Willie laughed and nodded and made her a sign of good-by.

The pleasant stillness of the evening fell around her like a blessing as she went on. Fireflies were filling one field, as if a conflagration under that particular ground sent up endless streams of sparks. She smelled the budding elders, and was reminded of tile-like bits in her past, fitted oddly together.

Morton lived but a few steps beyond the village. She had been talking a mere moment with Nancy Ellen, and had not yet entered the room where the preacher lay when another neighbor came in with excitement, and said aloud, over the whispered talk of the mourning house, that something was wrong down at the station.

"That express has run into something again," proclaimed the neighbor, "and looks, by the way folks run, as if it was n't a cow this time. Enough cows and pigs has been killed by that railroad."

"I have n't seen the express," said Mrs. Harbison, feeling her head full of wheels. "It was all quiet when I was there a minute ago."

"The express has stopped. Good reason! There 's something on the track, I tell ye," insisted the neighbor.

Willie's mother was sure it could not be Willie. He was conscious of his infirmity, and so cautious that she had long ceased to be anxious about him. He knew the times of all the trains with nice exactness, also. Yet she started from the house without speaking another word, and ran until she reached the crowd.

The engine stood hissing ; it confronted her with the glare of its eye, a horrid and remorseless fate, ready to go its way with bell-clanging and all cheerful noise, no matter who had been ground under its wheels.

The conductor was just stepping on board, for time and orders wait for nothing, The engineer had already climbed back to his cab ; he saw a running woman kneel down on the platform and draw the boy up from the boards to rest in her arms. Having seen that much, the engineer turned away his head and wept out loud ; and the train moved on, bearing pale faces that looked

backward as long as they could discern anything.

Mrs. Harbison had stumbled over Willie's
bent wheel first. When she found him indeed laid in the midst of the crowd, she did
not believe it. He was not mangled. His
bones were sound — she felt them with a
fiercely quick hand. There was no mark
about him excepting a dirty-looking spot on
one temple.

" Willie," she cried, shaking him.
" Willie ! Willie ! "

" We 'll have to carry him home," said
her husband at her side, his voice sounding
far off as if it came strained through some
dense medium.

She looked up, and could not understand
it.

" He 's knocked senseless," she claimed.
" Why does n't somebody bring water ? "

" He never knowed what hurt him," cautiously said one villager to another. " The
train was goin' so fast, and he come up from

among the houses onto it so fast, that it was done in a flash."

" And I don't never want to see no better boy than Willie Harbison was," responded the other.

But only his mother — when she had him at home lying in that pomp of death with which we all shall impress beholders — could have pronounced the true oration over him. Through her dumb tragedy she wanted to make deaf-mute signs to some intelligence that here lay one of Nature's poets, with a gift virgin and untarnished.

He had never hunted a public. His public was the woods and sky, and his critic one fond woman. Not a line of unsatisfied ambition marked his placid face. He had lived an humble, happy life, and sung for the sake of expression, not for the sake of praise. He had, after all, only gone to find the best publisher, and his mother could always hear him " singing in the dark."

T'FÉRGORE

A PASTORAL IN THREE PARTS

Time, 1883

PART I

HE THREATENS TO ARRIVE

"We will not endeavor to modify the motions of the elements, or fix the destiny of kingdoms. It is our business to consider what beings like us may perform : each laboring for his own happiness by promoting within his circle, however narrow, the happiness of others."— *Rasselas.*

"COME into the painting-room," said Julian, "and let 's talk it over."

"How excited you are!" I said.

"Well, after balancing one way and another for years, my mind 's made up. We 're going."

"To Europe?"

" Yes, to Europe."

" Oh, what a beautiful prospect," I said. And then leaning against his elbow I heaved a great sigh.

" It must be a beautiful prospect if you groan like that over it."

" The groan 's because I can't go."

Julian sat down and took me indulgently on his knee. Some women in marriage have their pride gratified by a good match, by all the pomps of life, or by unlimited allowances of spending money. But my portion is to be loved and cherished and fondled like an infant. I like it very much. Some part of me lingers in eternal babyhood. In the glass I frequently see a juvenile face with dimples around the mouth, that disowns its thirty years.

" You think," said Julian, after kissing me in a way which would scandalize some of the girls who made the best matches, " that we can't raise the money."

Such a thought would have been justified

by the fact that we seldom could raise the money.

"But we can. And what's the use of waiting around till we are old? I'm in my thirties. And if I ever do anything now's the time to do it. A man can't make a success of painting here in the west."

I looked all around Julian's studio. He had done many portraits, and hated them. They made our living. But he believed he was wasting time.

I always loved to be in the studio, and sometimes sat there a whole afternoon, with bits of sewing, behind a screen. A great many people took the elevator to explore Julian's work place. He had reputation in his native city. And when they stumbled around the screen on me, they might have taken me for a model. But most of the explorers were country people, piloted by their town friends to see the sights. I only looked odd to them. I know I looked odd, because Julian had me dress in loose gowns and broad hats. Cheese cloth is only four cents a yard and very wide, and with borders of velvet or lace it made sumptuous cool toilets. I was slim; and a dull blue gown, belted just under my arms and puffed at the shoulders, with an aureole of dull blue hat over it, made me look nice in Julian's eyes or I never should have had the courage to face the street. When a person is slim and lithe, however, her daring clothes have not the aggressive grossness of a fat woman's daring clothes.

Looking around the painting-room, I could not think Julian a failure. He had made it so pretty with tiles and pottery and draping stuff, and flowers painted in dull red or bronze vases, or in masses wasting their petals, and landscapes, some blurred so you had to squint your eyes to get the outlines. Looking at himself I always considered him a great success. His mouth and chin were so refined. He was muscular and alert in his carriage for a man of his profession, and his ideas were far grander than mine.

"So I'm going to sell the little farm," said Julian.

"Oh!" I exclaimed, "that's all the property we've got."

"Why, I thought you were perfectly willing. What does it amount to, anyhow? Fifteen acres and a scrubby house and barn."

"What will old Lena do?"

"Oh, she'll continue her gardening. I've had an offer of two thousand dollars for it. One thousand down, five hundred in one year, and the balance in eighteen months. We can live a long time abroad on that. And I shall get hold of something then. We'll never come back here."

I did not mind that at all. The prospect was dazzling. But I saw I should have to tell him at once.

"You didn't know your poor painter would take you to Europe, did you? Think of Rome, think of Paris, think of being domesticated in some ancient German city while I paint! "

" Oh, I think of it, Julian ; but could you go without me ? "

" Could I go without you ? " said Julian, setting me off on the tip of his knees. " Did I ever go to any place without you ? Did n't I manage that jaunt up to Canada with you ? Did I scour out to Colorado and leave you at home ? Do you *want* me to go without you ? "

" Oh, no ! "

" Then what are you talking about ? "

" I don't know."

" You certainly don't know," said Julian severely, " if you think I would go off to Europe for even a limited time, to say nothing of an indefinite time, without *you.* Why, you great baby, you 'd cry your eyes out ! And if you got sick who would do you up in packs and give you your medicine ? You can't get along away from me."

" I know it, Julian."

" And where would you stay ! " continued Julian with increasing indignation. " You would n't want to keep up a house, and you would n't want to board. And what business would you have over here by yourself, anyhow ! You provoke me ! "

" I believe I 'm going to cry," I said.

" I should think you would, for proposing such a thing. But don't do it."

" I *am* going to cry," I affirmed, and put my hands up to my face, while I quivered all over. These mute fits of sobbing, relics of my babyhood which I try so hard to outgrow, seize me unreasonably. They take away every scrap of dignity. I never could get the best end of a quarrel on account of this weakness ; for who could sweep out of a room with a stinging retort, when at the door she was sure to break down, lay her cheek against the frame, and sob until every fibre in her seemed melting !

The only good effect of my crying, besides

the delicious languor it left over me, was
that it melted Julian also. I have known
it to be a very convenient solvent when he
hardened himself into a male tyrant. His
face was sure to relax and his motherly
arms to gather me in. Some men will run
from tears, and very disagreeable men they
are. Julian seems to like the soaking. It
is tribute to him as a man, and certifies
to his grip on my individuality. He is convinced I am very fond of him, and depend-
ent on his gracious favor, when I creep to
his knees to cry.

Julian wiped my tears and comforted me
upon his shoulder, his face assuming its
usual superior expression.

When I got my breath and knew that I
could talk becomingly between little hic-
coughs, I told him the message I had from
T'férgore, and he saw at once how it would
prevent the European trip.

He whistled a minute, and we studied
each other's eyes.

" Well," said Julian, " I suppose we owe everything to the old fellow, and if he is really coming we'll have to prepare for him."

" Perhaps we better go out to the little farm," I suggested.

" Yes, I think we better. We'll have to economize, to gratify all his fastidious tastes."

" I wish he'd sent word to you, instead of to me," I burst out. " It's your relation this time."

" Yes, I wish he had," said Julian, smiling.

" Are you glad or sorry, Julian?"

" Glad, of course. But why did n't you tell me before?"

" How could I tell you what I did n't know myself?"

" Oh, it's his fault, evidently," said Julian.

I began to wonder if Julian would not be a little jealous of T'férgore. As I had never seen T'férgore myself, I did not know what

his aptitude might be at putting himself
forward and eclipsing the master of the
house. But I was glad it was Julian's relation this time.

We had had several of my kin living
upon our hearthstone at various times, and
though Julian was always kind, I think he
undervalued the stock from which I sprung.
He said I must have been changed in the
cradle, for refinement was my natural atmosphere. I did myself feel a creeping of the
flesh at brother Jack's ways; but the dear
boy had been brought up away from me, and
his manners were not his fault. He had an
affectionate and honorable nature, and soon
quit spitting upon our Brussels rugs and
hard finished floors; his English, however,
was beyond all help. I loved Jack so dearly
that it was a grief to me to see him falling
to pieces in his clothes, and slipping up and
down in shoes that were never buttoned.
He frequently put his trousers on wrong
side foremost, and came to me to help him

hunt the pockets. With my own pin-money I bought him hats that must adorn his rosy face, but after he slouched out in them once they looked disreputable. His coat-sleeves hung over his dirty fists like a hackman's. Whenever he passed through his room he left it as if it had been struck by a tornado. The earth adhered to Jack. Stray burrs and dumpings of gravel appeared by the chair where he sat to put on his slippers. He had no cattish horror of mud, and left the print of his foot on his napkin under the table. When Jack was partially dressed, he shouted for me, to the remotest corners, to come and button his sleeves and hand him his tie.

The more fastidious our company, the louder would Jack bite his nails, while he sprawled like a spread eagle on the sofa, until every pause in conversation became vocal with that horrible cracking. He lost everything portable which was not tied or buttoned about his person, but he was always so good-natured about the losses it seemed stingy to regret the money it cost to replace things.

As he had no inclination toward Art, and walked flat-footed over canvases whenever he came into the studio, Julian got him employment. Jack's apprenticeship to buying and selling was to me a long period of alternate hopes and despairs. He would begin well, and in fancy I saw him a merchant prince; but eventually he fell out with everybody and thought himself abused when his employer objected to his dribbling small change along the streets, and losing keys. I did not know what to do for Jack when the despair seasons came upon me. But in the end he did very well for himself. He got tired of the city, and no cajoling of mine could keep him from thrusting some shirts into a valise, grasping a pair of heavy boots in his hand, and starting for the country, sowing handkerchiefs and unmated socks in his wake. He went to work for a

middle-aged widow with considerable property, and she got the dear boy's consent to
marry him : so there he is, a landed proprietor, with a thrifty wife to button his
sleeves and join knives with him in the butter. Our bric-à-brac ways trouble him no
more, and what he loses in the furrow at
planting time he may find again during harvest. And when he comes to see us, his
loving heart is as mellow as the apples he
brings.

Then there was Aunt Lizy. I suppose
she was christened Eliza, but her name was
always pronounced Lizy with a plaintive
lingering on the *i*. We had her with us
two years. She was a stepsister of my step-
mother's. She looked like an Indian, and
had seen more trouble than any other woman with whom she ever measured experi-
ences. Her breathing was all done in sighs,
and she tweaked her nose so much it was
twisted at the end, and all of a dark red
color. She and I never could understand

why fortune hit her so hard, and we talked
about it so much that I was kept quite
bilious.

Aunt Lizy felt too low to sit in the parlor
unless dragged there by entreaties, and spent
a great deal of her time on the back stairs
with a sunbonnet drawn over her eyes.
She did not want to go anywhere, and the
sound of the door-bell exorcised her as if
she were a ghost. She compared her lot to
mine until I was ashamed of myself, wondering if I had not stood in her sun.

I think Julian secretly regarded her as a
trying disease that we had in the house, and
that must be doctored and endured. She
was so much in awe of him that I suffered
anguish with her whenever he tried to show
a man's bluff kindness to her.

Aunt Lizy finally died, and her face
looked young and cheerful in the coffin. We
scraped some money together and bought a
lot in the cemetery, and her misused body
rests there under roses, myrtle, and verbenas.

I take pains to keep her shade pleasant and her sod well trimmed; and when the flowers look particularly thrifty, I feel as if Aunt Lizy were learning how to laugh, at last.

Her daughter, who had been deserted by a husband as soon as she gave him a child to support, came to the funeral, and remained to make an unlimited visit and pick up such wearing apparel and other comforts as we had given Aunt Lizy.

She took entire possession of the house, being as loud-voiced and self-assertive as her mother was crushed and sensitive. But she owned me before everybody as her cousin, and took notice of Julian, though she preferred Irish society in the kitchen, and installed me as her nurse, while she enjoyed it. The baby's usual expression was that of a young bird when it hears the parent return to the nest with a full beak. I used to sit studying the interior of the poor child's throat, while its voice pierced my marrow. Julian made a sketch of the pimply little face, but finished it up with a black cat's body and a high fence. It cried steadily during its stay, and had the croup and the doctor and our sleep, until Julian said he must follow the excusable example of its father and abandon it. He paid the fare of Aunt Lizy's daughter to relations in the far west, and loaded her with whatever she fancied her mother's. Yet she probably thought we shirked kinsmen's duty toward her, for we have since heard the whisper that we got all that Aunt Lizy ought to have left her.

So I was glad that T'férgore and not one of my own stock now dictated a postponement of the foreign trip.

Next day we drove out to the little farm and saw old Lena. Julian declared she was worth driving the five miles to see, if it was only to say " Good-day, Lena," and watch her shriveled smiles. She always wore a blue calico or blue woolen dress, low shoes, and scarlet stockings. Her gait was a cheerful trot, but her tongue was lamest at the English language of any tongue I have ever heard. She had a grandson named Fritz, tallow-colored and blue-eyed, and covered with contagious smiles. He never had forgotten the feeling of wooden shoes on his feet, and clumped conscientiously in leather. Lena and Fritz rented the little farm, and Fritz pushed the vegetables, fruit, and butter to market in a hand-cart. Summer or winter, the road, a turnpike, was as smooth and hard as a floor. Every inch of the fifteen acres was under cultivation Such weeds as were allowed to grow had some medicinal property, or were good for feeding Lena's birds. She had her cages hung along the porch, the two canaries, the redbird, and the mockingbird trying to out-sing and out-chatter the wild things in the cherry-trees.

It was the last of May, and I snuffed delightful odors from the little farm. Nasturtium vines were already running up strings at the window. They produced little pods of which Lena made my favorite pickles. She had one blazing bed of tulips in the garden, and her early vegetables were showing green. Everything Lena tended grew like magic. Fritz had raked every stick and bit of trash into the meadow, and the heap was burning with a pale flicker in the sunlight, and raising smoke like incense from the sod. Whenever I smell that smoke I think I must tell my sensations to somebody who can put them in a poem: a homely poem about last year's pea-vines and strawberry and currant leaves, exhaling the dew as they turned into blue vapor, and suggesting, though I cannot tell why, the old home garden life when Adam and Eve were content to lean down to the sweet ground and feel the loam with their fingers, or take delight in the breath of fresh-cut grass.

The walk up to the porch was of uneven stones, each outlined by moss. Lena arose

between two gaping cellar doors at the side
of the house, and ambled down the walk to
meet us.

"Wie befinden, Lena?" said Julian.
"Suppose we put off that sale and you take
us to live on your prospective estate?"

"Was Lena going to buy it?" I exclaimed.

"Of course. She's grown so wealthy off
my land that she was going to turn me away
entirely."

Lena laughed and shook her head and
made gestures of good-will.

We went into the house, and Julian
bargained with Lena to take us home unto
our estate. There was plenty of room for
our furniture. Lena had nothing but a
spinning-wheel in one long slant-sided room
over the wing. Julian said he should leave
the spinning-wheel alone, hang his draperies
and pictures there, set up his easels, and
make it a painting-room. The house had
all sorts of tags and after-thoughts built to

the main part. Some boards in the floors arched downwards like inverted rainbows. You mounted two steps to one room and descended three to another. There were tall mantles and unexpected closets. The staircase twisted in a way I fancied T'férgore would not like. I sat down on the porch bench while Julian was giving Lena directions, and tried to picture T'férgore coming up the walk toward the house. Was he white or brown? Would he be churlish or full of the spirit of laughter? Was he bringing trouble or gladness to Julian and me?

PART II

WE PREPARE FOR HIM

"So many hours must I take my rest;
So many hours must I contemplate;
So many hours must I sport myself."

"Ah, what a life were this! how sweet — how lovely!
Gives not the hawthorn bush a sweeter shade
To shepherds looking on their silly sheep
Than doth a rich embroidered canopy
To kings that fear their subjects' treachery?"

" For trust not him that once hath broken faith."
King Henry VI.

" Against ill chances men are ever merry;
But heaviness foreruns the good event."
King Henry VI.

It took several weeks for us to get quite comfortably settled at the little farm. We lazily decorated our residence, or suspended labor upon it, just as we pleased. Then the delicious June days trod upon each other's heels. It seemed as if I had scarcely risen and found the breakfast Lena always kept for me — of toast and jelly and chocolate — before the evening star trembled in the west, and I was following her and Fritz to the barnyard to take my cup of new milk with the foam on. Even Midsummer Day, the longest and loveliest day in the year, was gone while we talked about it.

At first our friends came down from the city, but as the heat increased they took longer journeys. Julian painted zealously. He said after T'férgore came he would be hindered a great deal. I lay in a hammock

and watched him, sometimes wondering at
my new languor. I thought a great deal
about T'férgore, without talking of him to
Julian. Julian licensed me to be silly to a
certain extent: beyond that limit I kept my
silliness to myself. It was nothing for me
to twist Mr. Fergus Dering's name into
T'férgore, because I had a talent for re-
christening people and objects. But how
impatient Julian would have been with all
my speculations about T'férgore! I could
not make an image of him in my mind, yet
he was always haunting me. I wondered if
he would stay with us always; sometimes
his ideal head, with impalpable garments
below it, changing from expression to expression, laughed at me from the clouds.
What an individuality he must have to seize
upon me so before his coming! He was a
gifted creature, according to Julian; and his
silent approach was weaving me in a net-
work of fascination that I never thought at
first of resisting.

When I was roused to activity, we made haste to finish our arrangements about the house and get T'férgore's room ready. Julian himself hung some draping stuff from the studio there. We spent money on a bath, and a curious water jug and basin, and I could not feel contented without giving the chamber a more delicate look with muslin and blue silesia. We used to stand looking around this apartment with admiration. Julian hung one of his flower pictures there, though he said T'férgore would probably do nothing but make a face at it. And I never went into the woods for a handful of wild flowers, without filling T'férgore's vase of Dresden china, when I got back.

Then Julian said we must have a horse and vehicle, for if he knew anything about T'férgore that young gentleman would want to take the air on wheels. We had, however, very little cash to spend on such a turnout.

" We can dispense with style," said Julian,

" if a kind, serviceable rig is to be bought cheap."

So he kept a liveryman in town on the lookout for him, and one afternoon he received a message and went to drive home our bargain.

Lena followed me to the gate to see the flourish Julian described there before alighting.

" What made you get a cart? " I inquired.

" This," said Julian, " is a sort of a dog-cart. The rage is all for dog-carts just now, and we could n't have a phaeton, you know."

" But they are n't painted red."

" This one is," said Julian.

" And there is no place behind for the dogs," I further objected.

" Oh, well, T'férgore won't want to carry a dog," said Julian. " It 's a bargain on two wheels ! "

Whatever is mine acquires peculiar merits in my eyes. A halo of possession arches it, making it a little better than the same thing owned by anybody else. I accepted the red cart and followed Julian into the stable-yard, where, after Fritz helped him unhitch, he showed me the points of the horse.

" Women always notice the ornamental part of a turnout first," said Julian. " Before you looked at the cart you ought to . have taken in Leander."

" Is his name Leander ? " I inquired.

" So I have been informed," replied Julian.

" What makes him look as if he were crying ? "

" His eyes need sponging," said Julian. " This warm weather is severe on a horse's eyes."

" I hope he has not parted with any near and dear friend." " He looks as if he could hardly stand up under some affliction."

" Horses are dear now," observed Julian with severity, " and you can't expect to get a thoroughbred for forty dollars. The liveryman said he shipped a car-load to Louisville last week, some of them so weak they had to lean against the sides of the car. This one is sound, and only needs a little good care to bring him out."

" Yes, his bones all look nice," I assented. My heart began to warm toward Leander.

" It 's a fine thing to own a noble animal like a horse, is n't it, Julian ? — and to see him grazing around one's homestead."

Julian said he believed he would take Leander into the yard and let him clip off some of the grass, before stabling him.

Fritz put the red cart under a shed, and helped Lena milk, while we walked enamored after our purchase from one part of the lawn to another.

" What makes his hams look so sad, Julian ? " I inquired with concern.

" Flanks, you mean," said Julian.

" Yes. But are n't horses usually cushiony there ? "

" Pigs and prize cattle are," said Julian contemptuously.

"But his hind legs run up so tall that when he lifts one he seems to be coming in two, like Baron Munchausen's horse when it got caught in the city gates."

"Sorry you don't like him," observed Julian, scratching a match on his heel and lighting a cigar.

"I do like him, Julian. It would be strange if I did n't like our own horse! The way he is standing now does n't show his ribs so. Could n't we induce him to keep that position generally?"

But Leander now drew all his feet nearer to a focus, and frightened me by a convulsion.

"He 's just going to lie down," explained Julian. "He wants to roll in the grass. They say a horse that rolls clear over is worth fifty dollars, anyhow. Watch him, now."

We watched him in breathless suspense, Julian holding the lighted cigar away from his lips. Leander, after several half revolutions, brandished his heels triumphantly in the air and rolled clear over.

Julian and I shook hands.

" Gained ten dollars in value since I brought him home," said Julian.

Whatever doubts I had harbored about an artist's knowledge of horses certainly vanished. And Leander, after standing up to shake himself, lay down to try it again. But this time he brandished ineffectual heels and contented himself with only a half turn.

" Do you suppose he has gone off any in his value, Julian ? " I inquired anxiously.

" Not at all," said Julian, throwing out clouds of smoke. " You must n't expect too much of a horse on a couple of mouthfuls of grass."

We drove Leander a great deal during the July weather. The cart had very easy springs, and I liked billowing along on them, though the motion was a little jerky. Leander was a kind creature. He never kicked, though he sometimes got his legs tangled in

his tackling, fighting flies ; and notwithstand-
ing his countenance continued watery, he
took a widow-like interest in us. I fed him
lumps of sugar and bunches of very sweet
grass, which he swallowed in a resigned way.
Julian, with sleeves rolled up, zealously
mixed chopped feed for him, and Leander
smeared this from sunken temple to sunken
jaw, so that often when I entered the stable
I thought he was undergoing a poulticing.

Leander objected to railway trains, so we
knew he had spirit.

" There's considerable go in him," said
Julian as we trotted between fence - rows
where elderberries were spreading and ripening. " Wait till I get him fat once!
You 'll be astonished to see how he comes
out."

" Do you think his eyes will quit weeping
as his condition improves, Julian ? " I inquired.

" Naturally. We can get him glasses if
they don't," said Julian. " What an absurd

baby you are in your demands! Beauty
and muscle never go together in a horse.
Some of the best goers on the turf are a
mere mass of wires when you look at them
from an æsthetic standpoint."

It was really enough to have any kind of
power, except our own, trundling us along
the pleasant roads. I grew to feel no solicitude whatever about Leander's ribs while he
stood cooling them in the creek, and Julian
and I in the high cart watched the sunlight
come down the woods' aisles, and long festoons of grapevine dipping and reflecting
their leaves in water. When we met anybody I tried complacently to imagine we
were an English farm-couple very well to do
and what they call smart in our turnout;
or that we were Italian peasants, basking in
the sun as we jogged royally to some festa.
But Julian became very critical on the proportions of horses and vehicles to each other.
He ridiculed a combination of tall horse and
low phaeton, the top of which barely reached

up to the horse's back; or of pony and double-seated carriage, looking like a tug drawing a steamer. In short, we were satisfied with our own goods and chattels: and when Julian graciously lent Lena the turnout to go to town in, and she filled the cart bed with ripe tomatoes and the seat with her blue person and Fritz, its perfect adaptation to her uses convinced me what a versatile and valuable bargain ours was.

The time came for me to meet and bring home Jennie Purdy from the Avenue station. She had been one of my special chums at school. I always loved women; there seems to me something unwholesome and unsound in the woman who proclaims that she hates and distrusts all of her own sex. At school I was Jennie Purdy's easily-moulded slave: she dictated what I should wear and how I should conduct myself. I denied myself many a game of croquet, when that pastime was fresh, to sit and fan her while she slept off some slight indisposition. And in return she petted and instructed me in all the niceties of etiquette. She was half a dozen years my senior, and at that time enjoying a small fortune of her own; but this was afterward lost, and she had many a struggle before deciding upon and mastering the profession of medicine.

Jennie Purdy was one of the most fastidious creatures alive, an epicure, and unsparing of herself as a student. Years did not age, but rather ground her down to finer delicacy. I felt considerable pride in her, and counted on having her at hand when T'férgore came. She did not lack the eccentricities which always cluster around any woman living outside of intimate family life. She professed to dislike men; but I, knowing her warm heart, knew also her self-deception. All isolated women fall into one of two errors about the opposite sex: they count mankind a vast monster, to be avoided and suspected, or a vast angel to be worshiped in secrecy and silence; whereas, men are only good, comfortable souls, very much like ourselves, but made a little stouter so they can hold us and spread out their shoulders for irrigation when we want to cry.

Though Jennie Purdy held dark views of mankind, I suspected that under the surface she was one of the worshiping ones. Still, I was not prepared to have her tell me, an hour after our arrival at home, that she was on the point of marriage.

We sat down in T'férgore's room, where I had been showing her the appointments, and I pulled a hassock to her side, eager for particulars. She should be married from the little farm instead of a boarding-house, if she could be content with such a wedding as we could give. But I upbraided her for keeping her secret from me, almost as seriously as she once upbraided me for daring to marry at all.

"You won't want me to be married here," said Jennie, with a snap. "You'll have too many prejudices."

" But I always thought you were the person with prejudices, dear," I remonstrated, " and that Julian and I were too unconventional for you."

" I am going to marry a divorced man," disclosed Jennie.

I caught my breath and said " Oh ! "

" There — I knew it ! " observed Jennie.

" I did n't say anything but ' Oh.' What made him get divorced ? "

" You don't know him," said Jennie, " and so you can't judge of the circumstances."

" But you might try me," I pleaded. " Has he been divorced a long time ? "

" About a month," owned my old, fastidious chum, turning into another woman before my very eyes. She never was pretty, but a certain noble pride had given her a carriage I enthusiastically admired. Now she sat before me a dupe of her own absurd fancies, half defiant and half apologetic. The woman who had taught me that only most serious incompatibility should separate a married pair was going to wed a man who had been divorced one month!

" His wife was never a fit companion for him."

" Oh, no," I said.

" An ignorant, miserable creature, who entrapped him when he was a boy and has kept him down in the world ever since."

" It's always the wife's fault," I said.

" People were continually asking him how he came to marry such a woman."

" And he let the question pass without knocking down the questioner?"

" There never was anything fit to eat in the house, and his clothes were never fit to wear."

" Poor dear!" I observed. " Had his income anything to do with it?"

" She kept him from getting on," expostulated my old chum.

" And he brought all his grievances to you for redress?"

"I expected to meet nothing but preju- diced opposition in you," said Jennie. " But of course I was bound to tell you. You can- not say anything to alter my determination."

My head whirled with this spectacle of a sane woman suddenly gone mad over a worth- less man. Shakespeare never touched the weakness of womankind so closely as when he made Titania's infatuation. The greater the ass, the more Titania adores him.

" I hate such an irregular marriage ! " I said, breathing quickly.

"Yes, I know you do," retorted Jennie. " You 're the slave of society. You would n't have the courage to go against one of soci- ety's whims."

" I don't want that kind of courage which tramples on decent marriage customs. And you were the first to teach me the value of an irreproachable standing before the world."

" It 's easy for women like you, who know nothing of the miseries of an unequal marriage, to take a high moral stand," said my old chum, turning whiter always as our talk sunk lower. I was afraid Julian would hear us and come down from the painting-room overhead. He never liked Jennie as heartily as I thought it his duty to like her. And he laughed at the little barnacles of whims which an isolated life fastened on her.

All the time I was talking to her the fancied image of T'férgore was before my eyes.

" How much more faithful will this man be to you," I went on, " than he was to the woman he left one month ago ? He has somehow cast a glamour over you. I know just how he looks — a great, whimpering, Falstaffian baby of a thing, coarse to his last fibre ! "

" Go on," said Jennie.

" If he were not coarse would he ever allow a woman standing related to him as wife to be slurred to his face ? Would he be so ready to attach his mildewed life to yours without a blemish?"

" I can't hear you talk so," said Jennie. " You 'd better let me go away. I cannot stay in the house."

" You cannot go away," I declared fiercely. " I understand now why parents have locked their daughters up."

" You are interfering with what does not concern you at all," said Jennie, trembling, "and not in the least altering my determination. You cannot choose my fate for me. I have lived a lonely life year after year. Nobody considered me. Why am I to stand on nice points considering everybody? He thinks I can make him happy. I believe he will treat me kindly."

" You have every warrant for believing that," I exclaimed, struggling to calm myself in the fear that I was going to make a scene.

" I have," said Jennie, with a kind of pride strange in her ; " for he provided for the family to the full extent of his means, before separating from them."

" So he had children? And deserted them?"

" Five," replied Jennie in embarrassment.

" Five children! And he provided for them by taking their father from them when they needed a father most!"

" They are all boys but the youngest," said Jennie."

I knew now that I was going to make a scene, struggle against it as I might.

" And is the smallest a little child yet?"

" Not an exceedingly little child," said Jennie, picking at her dress and not seeming to see the fingers at which she stared. " Two years old, I believe."

" Don't you understand about family life? Don't you see what a callous wretch is the man who can abandon his own flesh and blood? How will you ever close your eyes in sleep again if you help him in wronging that little child — that little child!"

I stood up from my seat and groped toward her. The moment of my own weakness and terror was coming.

Jennie took hold of me as she used to do at school.

" I have spoken out to you," I said, hanging to her neck; "and now you must take care of me."

She saw that T'férgore was approaching the house; and her face filled with tender solicitude is the last thing I can recall as I fainted.

PART III

THE AMBROSIAL YOUTH

" His flesh is angel's flesh, all alive."
" Honor to the house where they are simple to the verge of hardship, so that there the intellect is awake and reads the laws of the universe, the soul worships truth and love, honor and courtesy flow into all deeds."

                                        EMERSON.

September weather was over the world before I felt able to be carried out of doors. I had been very ill, but at my worst I remember having Jennie on my mind, and hanging to her hand while I pleaded over and over the cause of the little child.

Now, though weak, I had reached a state of rapturous convalescence, and reached it quite suddenly. Julian lifted me out to the shaded lawn, where Jennie had wadded a rocking-chair with pillows. The leaves were turning, but none had fallen. Lena's birds hanging in a row along the eaves of the porch kept it up at a great rate, the canary seeming to recognize me and give me the name he had long since invented for me: turning his head and calling through the bars, " Maë, Maë! "

Lena and Fritz came around the corner of the house and grinned. Lena had saved the biggest pear on the dwarf tree for me, and Fritz brought a nosegay of marigolds, strong enough to stifle many invalids. " It 's quite like a Harvest Home," said Julian. " We ought to strap a corn-shock on Leander's back and lead him in the procession."

Then Jennie went into the house to bring out T'férgore. Jennie was not only my doctor, but she had turned up her sleeves and showed Lena how to cook the dishes I could eat. She had discharged two nurses, one after the other, and relied on herself and Lena's help, and Julian's solicitude.

" You never know what a woman is until you try her in a family crisis," said Julian, sitting down near me. " I was n't enamored of your Dr. Purdy before, but I 'll say this of her now: she has the coolest head, the readiest hand, and the largest fund of domestic skill of any woman I ever saw."

"I always told you that," said I in a superior tone.

" She 's stayed by us to the neglect of her city practice, I 'm afraid," said Julian.

" She is just getting into practice," I assured him, " and before coming out here announced her intention of leaving town for a change. It has been a severe change, though."

" But a man has been here importuning her about something."

I took hold of the arms of my chair. " What kind of a man, Julian ? "

" Oh, an ordinary person. Nothing striking about him. I thought he looked very sulky the last time he went away."

" Jennie was short with him, was she ? "

" She saw him only a few minutes each time, after the first, and I thought she was rather peremptory. There 's Doctor Theophilus again, and he 's footed it from the Avenue station. The Reverend never was so devoted to us as he has been since T'férgore's arrival," said Julian, smiling drolly.

I had a nervous dread of Julian's uncle ; he was the most respectable man who ever had the right to add Doctor of Divinity to his name. Large, broad, and ponderous, his mere presence seemed to reprehend the playful antics of life. I was afraid of his long upper lip, which shut as close as a snuff-box lid. His white neckties awed me, and the solidity of his choice words reproached me. Behind his back, and in spite of Julian's laughing remonstrance, I had rechristened Uncle Doctor Theophilus, whose surname was Marvin, The Old Daguerreotype. It is true he had not his case on, though the snap with which it formerly shut had probably passed into his lips. I could even fancy that when you got a side-light on him he retained the glare of the old daguerreotype, and effaced himself in a sheet of glitter. His expression seemed unalterably made up; and though he looked more ancient than other men of his age, I knew he thought himself well taken, and all his tints neat without being gaudy. He oppressed me so that I frequently wanted to rub him out. I always trod on a stone and turned my foot, or ran against a chair, when the Old Daguerreotype was by. Or he threw me into a nervous trance, and I sat with parted lips, glaring eyes, and aching neck, fancying that my own daguerreotype was being taken. Aunt Doctor

Theophilus used to be a worthy companion picture to him, but death years ago effaced her lineaments and snapped her case shut, . to be opened no more.

I felt that I could hardly stand the Old Daguerreotype just at this time, but said to Julian it was kind of him, taken in such a precise attitude as he was, to dust himself walking out from the Avenue, on our account."

" Oh, it is n't the first time he has done it," said Julian. " Something about our rural domicile has seized upon Uncle Doctor. He did n't go out of town this year, and he 's taking whiffs of the country between sermons."

" Between poses," I suggested softly. " I hope Jennie is n't bothered by his coming. She takes strong antipathies, and he does make one's backbone ache."

" Oh, she stands it," said Julian laughing, " affably, as if she were the artist who had taken him."

I turned around towards Jennie as Julian went to the gate to meet his uncle. She was bringing T'férgore across the porch and smoothing down the angel robes. She herself looked like a Madonna picture, pale and somewhat saddened, but most womanly, most touching.

"Jennie," I said, as she put T'férgore on my lap, standing before me to do so, "you have taken care of me as only a woman can, and pulled me through to paradise."

"Well," she replied quickly, "you took care of me first. I think I must have been out of my senses. But having this little monster to handle made things appear very different."

T'férgore blinked lazily, and struck out with ineffectual fists. The cherub-wings were perhaps hidden in folds of mull, but gazing on this wonderful creature's allurements, I was seized with a Saturn-like desire to bite and devour every flower-tinted atom. I forgot that the Old Daguerreotype

was at the gate, and worried my prey, breaking into a rhapsody of baby Romany.

In the midst of my Bess'ums and S'ee-
tums, and Old Dol'ums, Uncle Doctor appeared before me, and bent himself at T'férgore's shrine, with an expression nearly as
idiotic as my own. He clucked, whistled,
and snapped his fingers, and for one moment
I thought he was going to dance. But his
legs were taken too stiffly for that, and he
only limbered his entire length and cracked
the glass in a way which damaged him forever as my Old Daguerreotype.

Then he straightened himself up apolo-
getically and shook hands with Jennie, saying in his most ministerial tones, " And how
are you to-day, Dr. Jane? "

I must say that everything Uncle Doctor
did on this occasion astonished me. It was
the first time I had been permitted to see a
visitor, and they should have prepared me
for the unusual side-lights I should now
catch upon the Old Daguerreotype. He

held professional women in disdain, and I had heard him utter homilies against wives who tacked all their maiden or acquired names before their husband's cognomen. Yet here he was parading Dr. Jane's title, and almost capering before her in his exuberant desire to win favor.

They sat down around me, and I noticed how unembarrassed Jennie was by the Daguerreotype's white tie and the clip of his lips and fearful respectability.

" A little daughter in the house," said Uncle Doctor Theophilus, indicating with pomp the human atom in my lap, "is indeed a well-spring of pleasure."

" We counted on her brother Trotwood Copperfield, instead of his sister Betsey Trotwood," said Julian.

" It was a mere fancy," I insisted, "and girls are just as good as boys any day."

" Better," granted Julian.

"I'm quite as glad that T'férgore is a girl."

" But it disarranges the name," said Julian.

" His name was Fergus Dering, but I think we shall have to call her Ferguson."

" Not at all," I dissented indignantly."

" T'férgore ! " mused Uncle Doctor Theophilus. " What kind of un-Christian appellation have you stumbled upon there ? "

" The name being Fergus," explained Julian, " we call her — as Lena would put it — T'férgore in short."

We sat in silences of several minutes at a time, hearing an apple drop in the orchard, the call of the katydids, or the restless stepping of Leander in his stable. Already the smoky light of autumn was mellowing distances.

" How remote this little spot appears to be from the centres of traffic," said Uncle Doctor Theophilus, with a pulpit gesture.

" It 's a good place for fever patients," said Dr. Jane in a tone of authority. " There 's health in the air of the house."

" Yes, I should apprehend as much," asserted Uncle Doctor Theophilus.

"You mean the intellectual atmosphere, of course," said Julian, as a whiff of the sauerkraut Lena did love came around the house. "Oh yes, we are remote, but we have had great company here. Emerson has uttered wisdom from your chair, Uncle Doctor, and near him sat Hawthorne, and against that tree leaned Thoreau. We have even had what some fantastic literary fellow calls the tone poets all around us, and no end of painters and sketchers."

"It's nothing but a play of ours," I explained. "Whenever I wished we had such people for visitors, Julian piled chairs full of their books, or their music, or stood up copies of their pictures. Then we talked to them, and Julian read from them in reply, or I ran over the musical score, or he hung a picture where it could speak for itself. In that way he thinks we enjoyed just as close communion with them as their nearest friends ever had; because their elusive souls would speak to us more directly and coher-

ently than if they were sitting opposite us in
the flesh."

The Old Daguerreotype shook his head
indulgently over such pastime. On delibera-
tion, however, he said the next time we had
such a gathering he would like to join it.

After supper, and while Uncle Doctor
Theophilus and Julian were trailing their
feet through the grass, carrying their hands
behind them, and all but chewing the bovine
cud in their ruminative gazing on the bee-
hives, the orchard, the stable, and meadow,
Jennie put on her hat and gloves to drive
our relative back to the Avenue station. I
knew the drive would be good for her.

" You can come home the long way,
through the creek — the water is always low
— after you have left him at his train," I
hinted.

" I guess I shall go the long way," said
Jennie. " It will be pleasanter having some
one to talk with."

T'férgore and I exchanged a long stare;

that is, I exchanged a long stare with T'férgore for a series of self-absorbed blinks.

" I am so glad," I then remarked to Jennie, " that you are n't put out by the old
Dag — Doctor ; when I say old, I mean, of
course, reverend ; for he is n't really elderly,
you know."

" He does n't put me out a bit," answered
Jennie. " He is very quieting to me. I
believe he is a sound man."

" There is no man sounder," I declared.
" And he was just as good as he could be to
his wife. I think she actually died because
there was nothing more she could ask of life.
I never saw such a self-satisfied expression
as she had — outside of a miniature. His
position is excellent and influential, too. A
woman can't help looking at that sort of
thing when she is once married."

Jennie turned about to face me, smiling.
" Now, don't, my dear, don't," she objected.
" Let us not give our talk any such bias."

" Oh, I won't," I exclaimed apprehensively.

" I 'm not throwing anybody at you at all.
I was just going to say that though he is
such an excellent man, and near to Julian
and all that, he ossifies the working of my
joints : I feel in such awe of him."

" I don't," said Jennie.

" Yes ; I 've noticed that."

" I think his society is wholesome for
me."

" Yes ; it seems to be mutual," I could
not help suggesting. " Either you or T'férgore is limbering him up until I do believe
in the course of time his presence will become wholesome for *me*."

Leander, drawing Jennie and the Old
Daguerreotype in our red cart, went briskly
down the road, and Julian and T'férgore and
I sat watching them.

" They will loiter through the woods,"
mused I, " and watch the festoons of grapevine, and get a sniff of sycamore leaves and
pennyroyal mixed with loam."

" Yes," said Julian. " Next week I shall

take you and Ferguson off through the wood-
siest drive of them all."

. "Julian," I remonstrated, "her name is n't
and it never will be Ferguson."

"Oh, well," said Julian, "the bill is laid
on the table then. Another motion will be
in order."

"And they 'll see bunches of goldenrod
in a thicket," I continued, returning to
Leander's load, "and the Old Daguerreotype will jump out to get it for her, footing
it lightsomely among the burrs."

"You make quite a beau of our uncle,"
said Julian, turning his cigar over.

"Well, I should think anybody could see
that 's what he wants to be considered."

"He has my consent," said Julian.

"Mine, too," said I, taking high grounds;
"but I 'm not so sure about Jennie. She 's
a woman who has been hard to suit. Nothing
else stood in the way of her marrying long
ago."

I looked keenly at Julian, but he evidently

knew naught about the one month divorced man with a wife and five children — the youngest two years old. It was the only secret I had ever kept from him, and it burned guiltily at the roots of my tongue. But the woman who reveals to her lord and master some unlovely weakness of her own sex helps him to a judgment-seat too dangerously lofty.

"She's what you may really call superior," admitted Julian, "but far enough into the woods to be afraid of the crooked stick. And Uncle Theoph. is n't so bad."

"No," I granted generously : "he does n't make me half as miserable as he used to. And I know he won't mind getting bugs down his neck and stumbling over old logs for yellow and chocolate colored pawpaw leaves and branches of fire-red maple, if Jennie wants him to."

"I wonder," Julian ruminated, "if Aunt Marvin ever made him dance around when they were young together and she had a ribbon headdress on her hair, and he choked himself with a stock."

" No," said I, " she was his first wife."

Julian reached over, at the risk of waking T'férgore, and laid his arm across my shoulder.

" Besides, she never cried," I added. " And a good husband is just like a growing crop: he needs to be rained on."

Julian uttered a little grunt of contempt, but it was the kind of contempt which magnified the importance of his own sex and therefore did no real harm to ours.

" Uncle Doctor Theophilus is lonely," said Julian, " having once lived the life of a family man."

"And Jennie is lonely, too," I admitted, " having never lived the life of a family woman. Think hów hard it is to stand outside of — say the little farm — and see T'férgore come home, and our comfort and satisfaction."

" Man : his wife : his child : " ruminated

Julian. "The family; the little spot of our own ground. That 's the primitive and true life."

We heard the creek frogs lifting up their voices.

"Next summer when T'férgore is big enough to be carried across the field," said I, "I will make a Kate Greenaway dress with a yoke, and flare a hat of muslin for her, or better still, pucker her face into a frilly cap, and set her down in the midst of the clover where there are n't any bees."

"And put a crook in her hand," said Julian. "For now we are her sheep. We can't stray across blue water until the shepherdess permits."

ILLINOIS

BEETRUS

TIME, 1881

" BEETRUS JENKINS ! " called the owner
of the name, sending her high clear voice
through the boxed space which served as
post-office window.

" Yes, 'm," responded the postmaster, with
that joking freedom which adds so much
spice to the life of a general-storekeeper at
a South Illinois railroad station. " Three
letters this time. He 's writing nearly every
day."

" It wears on you to keep track of my
correspondence, don't it ? " affirmed the girl,
taking her letters and rending them open
with impatient forefinger. They were all
addressed, in the same mercantile hand, to
Miss Beatrice Jenkins, Wabash Station, Illinois. She compared the dates of the post-

marks, and opened the earliest, standing by the door to read.

The smoke-dimmed interior of the store was hung with baskets, dry-goods, bacon, ready-made clothing, and boots and shoes. A skeleton flight of steps ascended across a background of wall to the proprietor's residence, and up this flight of steps went a neighbor's barefooted child with a coffee-pot to borrow some household necessity, while Beetrus read her mail.

She was a spot of mellow color betwixt brilliant autumn tints outside and the dim inclosure. The slim, long-fingered hands holding her letters were nicely gloved. Her white hat was covered with plumes just owning the salmon-pink tint of her small woolen shawl. Her dress was neutral and unobtrusive. Not so, however, were her black eyes and glowing cheeks, or the dark hair clustering to her ears. She was a very pretty girl, and this the station-master always mentally admitted. He came out of his post-office cubby with the mail-bag in his hand.

"So you're going to clear out to-day, Bee?"   .

She glanced up, perceptibly starting and coloring.

"Goin' by rail or by river?"

"Oh!" said Beetrus. "Yes, we're going up the river. Our things are packed on the White Dove. We'd have to go so far around and pay so much freight the other way. But I don't like to go on a freight boat, and neither does ma, though the men are just as kind and clever as they can be. We have to sit upon deck all night, too, among the machinery and grease."

"Yes, you will. It's a twelve hours' run betwixt this and New Harmony against the current. The White Dove starts about three o'clock Will you be down any during the winter?"

"I guess not. Our man and his wife can tend to everything on the farm. We never do run back and forth any after cold weather sets in."

" And I suppose you 'll put the time in dancin' and takin' music lessons ? "

" It is n't so very lively in Harmony ; but I 'm going on with my music — That is n't the train ? "

" Yes, it is," responded the station-master, swinging the mail-bag as he walked forth to keep appointment with the black and hissing locomotive sliding to its brief pause.

Beetrus flew through the store, ran down the back steps, and sheltered herself in woods which stretched away toward the Wabash. Swift as her exit was, she scarcely escaped the eye of a young man who swung himself off the train, sample case in hand. His face twinkled humorously, which it could very well do, being a pleasant mustached face in spite of the marks of dissipation it bore. His trim dress and brisk air bespoke the prosperous commercial traveler.

He went indoors and swept a business-like glance around before the train steamed away; therefore by the time the station-master had put up the mail and served one or two customers, he had a satisfactory order written out, and professed himself ready to mount the next train, for which he would have to wait quite two hours.

"Oh, you know how to put the time in," said the station-master, "as long as we have any pretty girls left in the neighborhood."

The drummer smiled out of the back door at a huddle of two or three cabins and board huts, as if the capacity of such a place for producing pretty girls was too contemptible a joke for him to meddle with. He said he guessed he would go down to the landing and see if he couldn't get a skiff a while.

"Bee Jenkins will be down that way," suggested the station-master. "She was in here a minute ago."

"Ran from me," noted the drummer.

"I'd kind of advise her to, if she hadn't," said the station-keeper.

" What 's the objection to me ? " laughed the drummer ; " I 'm only a good gray sinner. They 'll have to dip me several times more before I 'm as black as you South Illinois Egyptians."

" Old lady Jenkins will have a crow to pick with you, though, if she happens to drop onto all these letters and walks."

" You undertake too much," said the drummer, shaking his head with gentle persuasiveness. " The store and post-office and station and the neighborhood will accumulate, and be too many for you."

Beetrus saw him sauntering on her track. The blood was buzzing in her head, and she hid herself upon a pile of steep high rocks, obeying some wild impulse of which she felt ashamed. To follow him with her eyes and be herself invisible was an impersonal rapture in which she could indulge without giving it too great advantage. Yet, when he disappeared near the river, she felt a stinging check in her heart, and a sense of having inflicted loss and robbery upon herself.

To Beetrus he was the walking essence of the world, representing not only its mighty business, but its advantages of culture and travel. She never had been from home except to Evansville and New Harmony; and he never stayed two nights in a place, and spoke with fatigue of his exciting life. What operas he had seen! — for in Beetrus's chaotic imagination all theatrical performance was opera, and operas were the distinct possessions of the worldly.

She resented with a mixture of awe and daring the greatness of his relatives. He was a nephew of the head of his commercial house, and his grandfather had been a congressman; while her background was the pioneer's cabin, the pecan woods, and Wabash rocks and hills.

Beetrus was the child of a shrewd though romance-soaked mother, who had dowered her with something more than a mispronounced fine name and biased imagination. It is strange to think how large a human mass, moving this instant in grooves of practical action, is protesting with secret scorn against all its conditions. Beetrus was full of a girl's unrests and eccentric impulses. She thought she knew exactly what she wanted for her happiness.

She pressed her cheek against the rock lichens, taking a half-inverted view of the autumn tangle, and glad in spite of herself for the pleasant breath of life. It was worth while to be a part of such woods and river vistas, and to smell all the ground's odors. Some little living thing ran along a log not far from her; and she could hear a squirrel bark, a whish and a whisper of loosened leaves as they were sent adrift, and then the dropping of a nut. Strong as the sunlight was, she shivered upon the rocks, and then felt all her blood burn, beat, and tremble.

The commercial traveler was walking back with a brisk step from the river, and scanning every opening among the trees, as

if on an eager search. He saw Beetrus rising and tightening her pink shawl on her
shoulders, and halted with a jerk.

" Where have you been? " was his un-
ceremonious exclamation.

" Up here, reading my letters and viewing
the country."

" You saw me go past, then, did n't you? "

" Was it you? " said she, fitting her foot
deftly to the steep descent.

" Let me lift you down. How pretty you
look this morning! "

" Oh! don't talk about pretty, Mr.
Poundstone," said Beetrus, dyed in color,
after he had stood her upon the moss, dazed
as she always was by his prevailing presence.

" You ought n't to have hid; I want to
talk up a scheme with you right off. It
popped into my head since I got off the
train."

" What scheme? " said Beetrus, hugging
her shawl and looking over her shoulder to
simulate complete indifference.

" You know well enough, or can guess. We must n't be parted, my dear girl; I can't run up to New Harmony every time I make a trip down this way. Think of the long winter. Don't you want to see me this winter ? "

" Oh — yes," she admitted, with a gasp.

" I want to see you. I want to have you entirely to myself, to look forward to every time I come in off the road. Let 's get married."

Beetrus visibly expanded and contracted with a great breath.

" Get on the train and go over to Evansville with me, and we 'll have the minister tie the knot there. Then home. And a nice little private set of rooms, all quiet and to ourselves, and no relations to bother us."

" But ma 's fixed things to go up to New Harmony for the winter," whispered Beetrus, struggling with this vision. " And she would n't change her mind so suddenly — 'specially as she does n't know you real well."

" It is n't ma I want to marry," argued Poundstone, using his winning smile. " I 'll drop my relations, and you can surely do the same."

" Drop ma ! "

The girl was stung by a covert insult.

" Leave her a little while. Let her go up to New Harmony, you know."

" And what do you mean about dropping your relations ? " demanded Beetrus, growing straighter and more self-assured, and burning more vividly in the cheeks. " That they would n't want to be acquainted with ma and me ? No, sir ; I ain't going to let her go up to New Harmony alone ; and I never would seriously have you unless she knew all about it and was willing. She might have read your letters if she wanted to ; she knows about them. I never did anything in my life that ma told me not to do."

" I thought five minutes' talk on this subject would bring you to reason," remonstrated Poundstone.

" Then you did n't calculate right."

" So it seems."

" I 'm not the girl you took me for."

" Do you want to break off with me entirely ? " he exclaimed, with heat.

" Yes — come to that — I do ! " cried Beetrus, flinging his letters at him, two fluttering uncertain, but one moulded by the grip of her hand and darting like a missile. " I believed in you, and see how you 've treated me ! "

" My darling girl ! "

" Don't you come around in my sight any more. And go marry somebody that won't cause any *dropping*. I can stand it."

" I believe you can," he sneered.

" Yes, indeed ; I can stand it. So good-by to you."

Saying which, Beetrus turned and scudded off, through Spanish needles and boggy spots, until his first half-uttered remonstrance had been for some time changed into language of another sort.

It seemed long before Beetrus found a log on which she could draw herself, face downward, with her arms stretched beyond her head.

The White Dove moved off from Wabash Landing two hours behind her appointed time. She was a dirty little boat, carrying a miscellaneous freight, but among the barrels on the after-deck some hard-favored and much-whittled chairs had been placed for Beetrus and her mother.

The young girl herself stood by the rope which served for railing, and saw her own heartache color all those fair distances. Downy swells of remote banks and bold juts of rock were copied in the river, so ruffleless did it seem to lie even when the strong current was moving. A blue heron stood at the water edge meditating, with one foot planted on sand and the other tucked up. It slightly spread its mighty wings, shook them, and folded them again to place, without appearing to break the trance of its downward stare.

While the White Dove churned along, shadows stretched upon the Wabash. Now it was very late afternoon, and now it threatened to be evening, with a hint that by and by it would be night, when you might expect the woods to make deep black borders along the river, and the canopy of stars to look smeared by the little steamer's smokestack.

When Beetrus was pale and tired, she turned and leaned against her mother — an ample, indulgent woman, who nevertheless had one bristling mole upon the right side of her face. She broke the tacit silence in which they had begun their journey by declaring, " Ma, I love you."

" You don't often put a body out telling them that," responded Mrs. Jenkins, uttering a gratified laugh.

" I keep up a dreadful loving, though," said Beetrus, casting sidewise at the river black eyes which swam in waters of their own.

" You 're my baby," cooed her mother, pat-

ting the slim hand fondling her neck.
" There's plenty of pretty young men in the
world, but there's only one old mother."

" I don't care anything about the young
men," said Beetrus, with strong scorn. " I
was thinking a good while in the woods to-
day, coming from the post-office, and I 've
made up my mind never to get married."

" You 'll turn around often enough before
the time comes."

"I never will," emphasized Beetrus. "We'll
be two nice old ladies together, ma, and neither of us will get married."

" I won't, for a sure thing," laughed her
mother. " But you 'll only be middle-aged
when I 'm ready to totter."

" Yes, that 's so," said Beetrus sadly. "And
then if one would die and leave the other "—

" Now, now, don't you fret, lovey. I 've
had consider'ble trouble and experience, and
if I don't sigh round, you need n't. Who 's
that nice-looking man that keeps looking
back this way? "

Beetrus had been facing down river, with her mind completely closed to any moving figures on deck. She glanced back over her shoulder.

" Why, it's "— she exclaimed, swallowing her breath with a gasp — "it's Mr. Poundstone."

" That correspondent of yours ? " said Mrs. Jenkins, nodding her head, and inspecting him sincerely with such thoroughness as intervening barrels permitted.

Beetrus's ears rang. She had, however, that instinctive western courage which sometimes takes the place of disciplined self-control; so by no other clue than the deepening fire of her cheeks and eyes did she give Mr. Poundstone any knowledge of the disturbance he brought her when he climbed a passage over impediments and placed himself in the party.

His manner was subdued, even becomingly humble and conciliatory.

" Ma, this is Mr. Poundstone," said Beetrus, secretly triumphant in being free from the subservience which yesterday would have made her say, "Mr. Poundstone, this is my mother."

She did not add to her unconsidered formula now, but allowed him to lift his hat and bow over her mother's hand.

"I'm glad to meet you, Mrs. Jenkins," said he. "I want to make friends with you, and get you to convince your daughter I'm not such a bad fellow as I look."

"You don't look like a bad fellow," she responded heartily.

"I didn't know you were going up on the boat," said Beetrus, regarding with gentle indifference the brim of his hat, after he replaced it.

"You know I couldn't go off on the train and leave matters in the shape they are. I never sold a bill of goods in New Harmony in my life, but I'm going to try to make a satisfactory trade for myself now, if the house turns me off for it."

Beetrus parted her lips smiling, and this
time met him in the eyes.   Without formu-
lating the fact, she knew there was sterling
man under the crust of acquired coarseness.
The brutal plan he had formed concerning
her, and which he was now scarcely willing
to acknowledge to himself, began to withdraw
from betwixt them like the mist which already wavered on the hills.

" I believe it will be a clear day to-morrow," the girl said, falling back upon good
commonplace.

" Do you believe it will be a clear day to-
morrow, Mrs. Jenkins? " inquired Poundstone.

" Well, it seems like it might be pretty,"
responded the widow, turning up her face to
see the pinkness reflected from the west.

" Then I believe it will too," said the commercial traveler, with a devout air, which was
unmoved by Beetrus's laughing out, —

" A great deal prettier and clearer than
to-day has been."

THE BRIDE OF ARNE SANDSTROM

Time, 1885

" Big Swede wedding over there this evening," said one passer to another by his side. " Peter Lund's daughter."

" Is she marrying a Swede ? " inquired the second.

" Yes ; fellow by the name of Arne Sandstrom."

" I should think old Peter, well off as he is, would have looked higher for a son-in-law — you or me, for instance," observed the second youth, with a laugh.

" The girl's pretty as a pink, and has had every advantage. It is a pity to see her thrown away ; but old Peter has a lot of younger ones coming on."

" That makes it less an object. I thought she was his only. The Swedes are clannish."

" Peter Lund's is headquarters for them, too. Here's one now, hunting up the wedding. I'll bet she's just arrived from the old country."

So near the truth was this surmise that Elsa had been off the train only twenty minutes, and in that time had repeated the name of Arne Sandstrom interrogatively to every person she met. She was dazed by long riding and partial fasting, and the dumb terror of finding no one to receive her at the end of her great journey. The letter created with much brain-work to announce her coming ought to have been in his hands weeks ago. The innocent and friendless soul did not know she had omitted all dates and exactness in her general care for spelling and inky loops. So stepping off the train into the American town at dusk, she saw stretches of summer prairie to the westward, perky architecture, crossing railroad tracks, hurrying citizens, and lazy loungers — even the new electric light on its spiderwork iron tower beginning to make a ghastly powerful star far above her head. She saw baggage and piles of express matter, hotel runners, and other women, starting toward their assured homes, tucked laughing and chatting under their husbands' arms ; but she saw not one face or one kind hand ready to bid her welcome, who had ventured thousands of miles alone — across ocean, across continent — to marry her betrothed lover, Arne Sandstrom.

Hearing his name spoken, she stood still upon the sidewalk, shrinking and timid, but directly in front of the young men, and inquired, using hands and eyes as well as anxious inflection of voice, " Arne Sandstrom ? "

" She wants to know where Arne Sandstrom is. Right over there — that big house, which you see lighted up. She does n't understand. Arne Sandstrom over there. Getting married ! Yes, yes. Arne Sandstrom. Here, Jack, you trot out a little Swedish, can't you? You 've been among them more than I have."

" Arne Sandstrom *derover*," exclaimed the other, pointing to Peter Lund's house, with a fine assumption of handling the language well. " Arne Sandstrom *jifta* to-night, you know."

" Yifta ! " said Elsa, shrinking down in stature.

" She 's got hold of it. That 's all right. You 'll be in time for the wedding."

" She did n't understand ; she thought we were making fun of her," said one of the lads as they sauntered on.

" She did understand, and there she goes straight across the street. Brush up in the languages, young man, and make yourself as useful to the public as I am."

When Elsa had entered the Lund premises, however, she did not ring the bell, but wavered around the house, looking up at lighted windows, and shifting her little bundle from one arm to the other. She had

other baggage at the station, but it seemed
no longer worth while. There was a western
veranda, on the lowest step of which she sat
down in quiet stupor to collect herself for
some determined movement.

Anguish and disappointment must be the
natural lot in this ·world, only she had not
lived enough years to find it out before.
Though summer darkness had come, the
after-glow was still so bright in the west that
it half quarreled with abundant lamplight.
Elsa could hear the front gate, the crunch of
coming footsteps, and frequent peals of the
door-bell, as she sat drawn together, and the
eternal minutes traveled on.

Peter Lund's house was full of joyful stir.·
China and silver tinkled in the open dining-
room, where several women were putting last
touches to the tables. Girls flew up and
down the back stairway, calling to one another in Swedish.

" One thing is sure, Yennie Yonsen,"
called a voice in the home tongue, " there

will not be enough married women to take
the bride from us girls in the wedding dance;
so now what will Arne Sandstrom do?"

Three of them conspired together by the
western dining-room door, bobbing their
flaxen heads, all laughing and talking at
once in their light happiness, far above the
unseen stranger on the step.

"Who told me Arne Sandstrom left a betrothed girl in Svadia?" said one, lowering
her voice to graver colloquy.

"Oh, well, she married, herself, of course,"
replied another; "and any man who could
get Lena Lund would take her."

"Lena's so pretty."

"Lena's rich."

"Lena can sing and play better than
some Amerikanskä."

"Lena has ten new dresses. Arne will
not have to put his hand in his pocket for
many a day."

"She is not spoiled therewith. I always
liked her."

" Ah, my mother said if this wedding was going to be in Svadia this St. John's Eve, what a night we would make of it ! "

They ran away, while Elsa repeated to herself that this was the Eve of St. John — night of arbors and rejoicing at home, night when the sun scarcely went down, and everybody feasted and visited under green-leaf tents. Of what use was St. John's Eve, or any other portion of time, to a girl put to shame and despair as she was ? Why had Arne Sandstrom sent her money to come over with if he meant to jilt her on her arrival ? Or had he picked another betrothed for her as well as himself ? She would not believe her Arne could be so evil; she would knock and ask for him. He was so kind ! he loved her. Yet not only the Amerikanns, but those laughing girls, had said plainly this was Arne Sandstrom's wedding; any man would take Lena Lund who could get her ; Lena was so pretty ; Lena was rich ; Lena could sing and play better than some

Amerikanskä; Lena had ten new dresses, and she was not spoiled.

Elsa bruised her cheek against the edge of the second step above her. She did not know where to go, and her money was all spent except the little she had saved by going without food during part of her railway journey, and she had saved that to buy some little ornament for her new home with Arne. She might try to hire herself out, but how could she ever write back home where such happy news was expected from her, or how could she put unendurable anxiety upon those best friends by not writing at all? Svadia was so pleasant, especially in the long nightless summers. Good and kind they were to strangers there: her mother always baked waffles and carried them with coffee to the morning bedside of a guest. She could see her native meadows stretching away in the blue northern air, and the iron whip, as her mother called the scythe, beating up an appetite in those who wielded it, while she her-

self, a careless little maid, came bearing the
second breakfast to the mowers.

A quavering but hearty voice, which
might have come from the mouth of her own
grandmother if it had not belonged to Peter
Lund's mother, sung out a Lapp-Finn nurse
song by an upper window, and Elsa knew
just what syllables the dancing baby was
made to emphasize.

> " Donsa lupon,
> Hopsom tup an,
> Lanti lira,
> Hopsom stira :
> Sprönti lupon, lupon,
> Hopsom tup an, tup an,
> Lanti lira, lira,
> Hopsom stira, stira."

> Dance and jump,
> Hop like a rooster,
> Hop like the skatan.

Perhaps this very instant — for Elsa made
no calculations in longitude and time — va-
der's mütter danced the baby under her home
roof ; and none of her people knew how

faint, how outcast, how bewildered the eldest child felt sitting on steps in a strange
Amerikanski town.

In Elsa's box of clothing was the finest
sheepskin blanket her mother ever made, so
white in fleece, and cured by buttering and
scraping until the skin yielded soft like
chamois leather. It was lined with scarlet
flannel. She could see the storeroom of her
father's farmhouse hung thickly with such
fleeces, and hear her mother say she wished
Elsa could take more, since they had so little
money to send with her. But Arne Sandstrom had sent the money to pay her way,
because he loved her so. They were children together, and he was held as dear as a
son in her own family. Elsa's mother never
distrusted him. How could it therefore be
possible that Arne Sandstrom, after sending
for his betrothed, could be marrying a Swede
Amerikanskä fleka the very evening of her
arrival?

In her intensely quiet fashion the poor

girl was wiping away tears as fast as they dripped down her cheeks, and now she lifted her head from the step, coming to a decision.

She walked up on the veranda, her feet sounding heavy and uncertain, and stood at the door ready to knock. Her piteous great eyes moved from wall to wall of the ample dining-room, recognizing Svensk wooden spoons and beautifully painted and polished Russian bowls in various sizes on the sideboard. Hard-baked Svensk bread, so loved by the white and firm Scandinavian teeth, and all known home luxuries, with unheard-of Amerikanski things, smiled at her from the glittering tables. This Lena Lund would be called a mamzelle in Svadia; she was very much above a poor yungfrau like Elsa. Any man might be glad to marry her. Still Elsa would not believe Arne Sandstrom had forgotten his betrothed.

She could see him from where she stood, in an inner room with a background of fine furniture. How beautiful he looked, all in

Amerikann clothes, and with soft dark gloves
on his hands, like a very rich man! His
cheek was ruddy, his forehead white, and the
very round of his ear — how well Elsa remembered it! Arne Sandstrom was happy,
and laughing aloud with other people. She
heard his voice while she stood just without,
so wretched her whole soul seemed numb.

In perfect silence she waited, and still
saw him laugh and extend his hand to have
it shaken by one and another, until a figure
came out of the room where he was, to
pass through the dining-room, and she knew
in an instant Otto Jutberg, who came to
America with Arne. Elsa put her foot
across the threshold and said, to call his attention, " Otto."

Otto approached the door and looked cu-
riously at her. One rope of her flaxen hair
hung down on her breast, and she looked
travel-worn.

"Otto Jutberg, I want to see Arne Sandstrom."

" Arne is going to be married in a few minutes," said Otto.

" I know he is. But I want to see Arne Sandstrom. Tell him to come here."

" Who is it?" pressed Otto, coming nearer to her, and knitting his brows inquiringly.

" Don't you know me, Otto, when you have been to my father's nearly every St. John's Eve of our lives?"

Elsa felt that she needed only one more drop to her cup, and that for some voice to raise the derisive song with which her countrymen mocked Scowneys, or inhabitants of a region the butt of all Svadia.

"A Scowen, a Scowen " —

one bar was enough to rouse sudden rage in any Svensk.

But instead of " A Scowen, a Scowen," rising around Elsa's ears this enchanted night, such a din of outcries was made by Otto Jutberg that people ran to look into the dining-room, and then to swarm around her.

Arne Sandstrom leaped two chairs and seriously jarred one table, to receive Elsa in his arms, when he kissed her openly.

"Bring me one of the chairs I kicked over," he exclaimed, "and let me set the tired darling in it. I have been looking for the letter which would tell me when you intended to start. Yes, this is my Elsa," he announced, displaying her; "and how did she find her way in here alone? Mrs. Lund, Elsa has come!"

"Yes, and she has been crying," said the plump wife of Peter Lund, pressing her hand. "It was enough to break any child's heart to reach such a journey's end homesick and unwelcomed."

At this Elsa leaned against the matron's side, and shook with sudden sobs, feeling her forehead and hair petted by a good mother's palms.

Elsa was taken upstairs by both Mrs. Lund and Arne, who talked rapidly across her. She was put into a beautiful room, and young girls came to get acquainted with her. Arne asked her for that piece of metal which would redeem her baggage, and he handed it over to Otto at the door. Before she understood her position, or was quite able to lift her eyes and look at all who wanted to talk to her, the box which had borne her company from Svadia was brought in, and Arne told her the other wedding would be put off half an hour while she got ready. Then he drove the merry company out of the room, and stood with his back to the door to keep at bay that moment all volunteering bride attendants.

"Can you be ready in half an hour, after your long journey, my darling?" said he.

"I can soon wash off the dust and change my dress," said Elsa. "But, Arne, I do not know anything. Who is going to marry Lena Lund?"

"Arne Sandstrom. And you will be married at the same time."

"I thought that was what you and Mrs.

Lund said. But who is going to marry me?"

"*Who!* I am — Arne Sandstrom."

"I will not do it," said Elsa. "They never have two wives in Svadia."

Arne Sandstrom gazed silently at her, puffed and exploded his cheeks, and bent over, striking his knees with those delicately gloved hands Elsa had first noted with such awe. He roared in the fervor of his laughter. This American country had in no way abated Arne Sandstrom as a Norseman.

"Oh, Elsa, my snowbird, if I should tell this on thee they would laugh at thee from one end of town to the other. Lena Lund's bridegroom is my cousin Arne, that came over with Otto Jutberg and me."

"That was Arne Peterssen," affirmed Elsa.

"But there are so many Peterssens and Yonsens who take their names from their fathers' Christian names that Arne changed his to Sandstrom. It is a very common thing to do here."

Elsa laughed also. It was so simple and clear and Swedish she wondered that news of Arne Sandstrom's wedding had caused her even a misgiving. She left her chair to swing Arne's hands while they both finished laughing.

" But you ought to be ready," he cried, " and not keep the others waiting. I got the papers for the wedding when Arne got his papers, so there would be no mistake of names on the record, and so I could marry you as soon as you came."

Within the hour, therefore, Elsa was the bride of Arne Sandstrom, arrayed in her dark blue wedding dress of wool, and not shaming by her statue-like proportions and fairness the lighter prettiness and silken raiment of Arne Sandstrom's American Swedish bride. Happiness and love were, after all, the natural lot in this world, thought Elsa, sitting by her husband in her place of honor at the wedding supper, and tasting the first course of such a feast — the Swedish soup of rice, prunes, raisins, and molasses.

THE BABE JEROME

Time, 1892

THE civil engineer sat at breakfast with his sister. Their table was a stationary one, on stakes driven into the ground, and they drank their coffee from tin camp cups with hooked handles. But the cook served them with broiled fish and game stew, brown pancakes and honey.

The tree overhead was still wet with dew. Lilian had a scarlet shawl around her. She was a girl whose dark eyes and distinct eyebrows you noticed at once, adding afterwards to her personality hair inclined to cluster about the face, and a general elegance of figure which her camp dress suggested instead of outlined.

"As I was bringing my birds in," said the civil engineer, " I saw Jerome and his gander sitting on the top rail of a fence, side by side. Jerome had his neck stretched up, whispering to the sky, and the gander had its neck stretched up, hissing its meditations. They were a divine pair ! "

" As divine as Minerva and her owl, I should think," said Miss Brooks. " He seems to me a tragic figure. How can you laugh at him ? "

" How can you help laughing at him ? But I do pity the old father."

" And the blind aunt. Eric, I 'm going across the river to see her. I told Mr. Marsh I would, the next time he came to camp."

" He 's coming now. There 's his boat on the river."

Lilian watched the boat and the Wabash. The expanse of limpid water was so shallow in places that its pebbles glittered in the sun, or a sand-bar showed under the surface, while the current in its channel ran deep and strong. Woods clothed its banks, and a gauze of blue hung over its southern bend. Northward a bridge stood on mighty legs of masonry, screening the work of the engineer among rapids beyond. A flat-boat ferry was being poled diagonally across from the east shore to the west, having for passengers a farmer and his horse.

The approaching skiff grounded also, and Jerome's father stepped slowly out and came across a stretch of gravel and sward to the camp. Quantities of gray hair and beard, a stoop in his shoulders, and a staff in his hand made him venerable, yet his arms were strong and his eyes black and piercing. He was the richest man in his county, and the man most indifferent to externals. Over his jeans garments he wore a blue woolen cape edged with ancient gimp, evidently taken at random from women's clothing.

He saw with approval the camp appointments : the civil engineer's men breakfasting at their long table ; the cook moving in and out of a canvas kitchen ; and the young lady's tent, revealing a pink net-screened bed, rugs, and stout book-shelves.

" You 're right well fixed over here," he called out before the campers could wish him good-morning.

The engineer said he always tried to make his camp comfortable.

" And this is as pretty a stretch," continued the visitor, drawing nearer, " as you 'll find between New Harmony and the Ohio. But ain't it lonesome for sis here by herself all day when you and the men 's out ? "

" Our cook stays in camp," said Lilian. " He has lived in our family since I was a child. So I feel secure. The friend who was to have been my companion here was detained at the last minute. But I made my brother bring me, anyhow. Will you have some breakfast, Mr. Marsh ? "

" No, I 'm obliged: I 've e't. I come across to look after the Babe. He forgits to have his breakfast sometimes. Seen him on this side — the Babe Jerome? "

" He's in the woods with his white gander," said the engineer.

Mr. Marsh rested against the tree and braced himself with his staff.

" Billy's never far off from Jerome. The Babe gets lonesome on the river, like sis here, and that gander's great company for him. But the Babe likes to be lonesome. We still call him the Babe," apologized the old man, " though he's twenty-five year old; scarlet fever done it. He was the smartest boy on the river. I 'lowed to settle in Shawnytown, and send him to college. His mother was a scholar. Now there's nothing to do but let him play his music. He's a good babe. He never gives me no uneasiness except forgittin' his breakfast."

" Do you think he would breakfast with us ? " inquired Lilian.

" Call him," suggested her brother. " As for me, I must be excused. There's a big day's work to be done on that bar — time the men were in the boats."

Captain Eric caught up his broad hat, and flourished it in adieu. The cook ran after him with a list of needed supplies. Lilian watched him sitting with folded arms on his camp-chair in the stern of his boat, until the rise and fall of oars and the song of the men drew off to remoteness. She turned to speak to her visitor, and found Jerome standing with him.

" Want to go back over ? " his father inquired tenderly.

Jerome shook his head. His visible flesh had a porcelain quality, like the unstained clearness of infancy. His hair glittered in the sun, and he had a long golden mustache, parting in the centre and trailing down his mouth corners below his chin. So strong and manly an ornament sorted strangely with perplexed blue eyes, that, in spite of a puzzling world, laughed with the delicious joy of life. Jerome's head stood upon a column of slender body. His clothes, to which a few burrs were sticking, would have seemed too fine for his environment if they had not so exactly suited him.

"Lost his hat again!" bantered the father. "That's the fifth straw hat I've bought him this summer."

"If you will have some breakfast with me, Jerome," said Lilian, "I will go to your house and eat dinner with you."

"That's a bargain, ain't it, Babe?"

The Babe Jerome looked from one to the other, and smiled, and sat down. His gander, lifting and shaking both wings, quavered a remark and waddled to his feet.

"How white Billy is!" said the young lady, after the cook had brought fresh food and she had helped her guest.

"The' ain't a gray quill on Billy," observed Mr. Marsh, his bearded lips relaxing with contentment.

"And his eyes are blue — blue as the sky! His bill, with such funny nostrils in it, is the purest coral. I did n't know geese could be so beautiful. You pretty fellow! Will he hiss me?"

" No!" spoke Jerome forcibly, startling her as she stretched a timorous hand to brush Billy's plumage. It had satin firmness. The gander squatted on his webs and observed in his own language that the caress was agreeable.

Jerome left off eating and leaned on his folded arms to smile. He was a sylvan creature, strayed out of pastoral days into the hazy regions of the Wabash.

He rowed the boat back, his father sitting in idle comfort on the other bench, and Lilian facing the oarsman. She enjoyed the grace of his torso, the veins swelling on his hands, the steady innocence of his gaze, with the same kind of satisfaction given by a scent of sycamore leaves, or the exquisite outline of an island. Billy swam after the boat, the water curling away from his breast; and before it could be beached he had left his web marks on the home sands.

The Marsh double cabin, with central chimney hospitable enough to engulf thousands of swallows, stood on a low bluff. Another and more imposing house was rising near it. The workmen's noise mingled with stable-yard cackle.

"How I love to hear chickens!" exclaimed Lilian. "They remind me of some wonderfully good time I had when I was a child, though I can't recall it. You have all the cheerful racket on your side of the river. And how sweet the building wood smells!"

"Some of that's sweet pine," explained Mr. Marsh. "The Babe, he carries them chips, and sassafras bark, and spice-wood, and all kinds of woods things, in his pockets."

The Babe looked at Lilian, repeating slowly what he had told himself many a lonely day, in forest or on river, —

"I — have n't got — right sense."

"Oh, don't say that!" she begged.

The father's mouth corners fell into leather grooves.

"But Babe 's got idees," he maintained. "He takes to nice things. So did his

mother. I 'd have built the new house long
ago if she 'd lived. And I would n't build
it now if it was n't for the Babe. Betsey
and me like the cabin. We 'll miss the big
fireplace, and them hooks in the jice beams.
I took Jerome and Betsey down to Shawnytown to stay one winter, and I 'd 'a' died if
I had n't come back here every two weeks."

" This is a lovely spot," said Lilian.
" When you are really settled in your new
house, you will enjoy it more than ever."

" I don't know. It 's just as the Babe
turns out to like it. The cabin 's been his
cradle. If the new one goes against him
I 'll lock it up and bring him back home.
Come in," invited the old man, climbing
his doorstep. " Here 's Betsey will be glad
to see you."

From the smoked and chinked interior
groped a large woman so delicately and completely white that the blanching appeared to
extend through her eyes, for the lids revealed them colorless. She wore a black

net cap and a dress and a cape of faded
lawn. Her heelless soles made no sound
on the bare boards. The palms which she
spread before her had the texture of shriveled dogwood petals. The stirring of the
lawn clothes set free scarcely detected per-
fumes, — of apples, and mint, and the old-
fashioned roses which grow nowhere now
except in remote and dewy country gardens.

" It's the young lady from the camp,
Betsey, come to visit us to-day."

" That sounds heartsome," the blind sister responded. Lilian took one of her fluttering hands ; the other half unconsciously,
with the swiftness of custom, moved up the
girl's shoulder and passed over cheek and
head. Lilian noticed in what masses of
wrinkles this handsome old face hung, and
wondered at the miracle of age ; at the childish sweetness that comes back to toothless
talk. " I love to have the young around.
It's been missly in the house since Babe's
mother died."

" Well, take a cheer," said Mr. Marsh,
" and I 'll look into the kitchen and tell
Marthy Dempsey who 's for dinner. Marthy she keeps house for us, and she 's a good
cook ; she used to work in a tavern down at
Shawnytown."

Jerome lingered on the log step while his
father performed the sacred rite of seating a
guest. Aunt Betsey groped toward him.

" But where 's the Babe ? "

" The Babe 's as far in as he likes to
come," said his father. " The Babe 's great
for outdoors in summer time."

" The dew 's off the garden," spoke Jerome.

" He never disremembers my walk,"
chuckled the blind woman. " As soon as
the jew is dry he fetches my bonnet."

Miss Brooks herself tipped the sunbonnet
at a satisfactory angle over the black net
cap, so that its crown sighted the heavens.
Jerome helped his aunt to the ground, and
guided her around the house, his arm on

her waist. He glanced backward often, to draw Lilian along, and she sauntered close, glad to be a part of all this innocent life.

Woods stood at the rear of the garden, and abrupt Indian mounds ruffled their tufts of fern almost overhead. It was growing warm ; scarcely a trace of the humid morning remained, even under burdock leaves, which Martha Dempsey prized for her butter. There was a rank hot smell of marigolds in the sun, with a peppery addition of bouncing betties. The sweet-williams were fragrant as honey and long spikes of red or white hollyhocks swayed in the faintest of breezes. Aunt Betsey scented the camomile bed and picked bits of sweet-mary and basil for Miss Brooks. The sound of the workmen's hammers on the house, the rippling of the river, and the summer call of insects and birds filled the air, until it seemed to tremble over green distances with this weight of pleasant life.

There was a cherry-tree full of ripe black

fruit. Martha Dempsey came out bare-
armed, but with a sunbonnet pinned shut below her nose, and, with the unconscious arro-
gance of the country maid, ordered Jerome
to pick her some fruit for pies. He pulled
down the lowest branches and filled her tin
pail. Then his aunt and Miss Brooks sat
under the tree and had their laps weighted
with ruby globes on platters of burdock
leaves.

" I like cherries best of any fruit," said
Lilian, " and these rich red ones most of all.
They get a wicked clip on your tongue that
is delightful."

Jerome considered her, and said with conviction, " You look like a cherry."

" Then these tart fire-drops ought to be
my natural food."

" This is Babe's tree," said Aunt Betsey.
" He planted it, and it has growed with his
growth."

It was quite dusk when Jerome landed
Miss Brooks at the camp. Her brother
met her, and she exclaimed to him : —

"I have had a lovely day! And I persuaded Jerome to bring his violin and play for us a while. His playing is wonderful, Eric."

"So is Long John's singing," observed the captain with contempt.

From the men's quarters came an unmelodious shout of — "Injun puddin' and a punkin pie! O, Je-ru-sa-lam!" But this wavered and ceased when Jerome took up his violin. His fingers floated along the strings, and the score he played was never set down in any brain but his own.

The moon came up, and he played straight on, tilting his head back and smiling at floating films in the sky. The cook drew near from his tent, and the men, smoking, crept as near as they felt discipline would allow to the captain's quarters. Jerome, in the full beatitude of his one unspoiled talent, knew no audience. With a final triumphant cry of the strings, he got up and walked off without saying good-night.

" He can sling a bow ! " commented one
of the listeners. " They say around here he
plays the birds off the bushes."

" He is like a girl," said Miss Brooks to
her brother. " I enjoy having him about
almost as unreservedly as if he were a girl."

" Glad of it," replied the captain. " He
can pilot you through the woods. It's a pity
the poor harmless fellow is daft. He might
have been something."

Jerome came to camp every day, Billy attending him. Miss Brooks in her bathing
dress floated on the river, holding to his
boat ; and he kept a maternal eye on her
while she disported herself. He brought
her Indian hatchets, and arrow-heads, and a
piece or two of pottery left by the Shawnee
tribe. The two explored creeks and islands
to such extent that Billy frequently left them
in disgust. He snipped grass, and quavered
to himself, while Miss Brooks read or talked
to Jerome.

She talked to Jerome as if he were a rational being. His delight in the woods was even keener than hers, and his knowledge of wild creatures much greater. He taught her skill in fishing. His joyful father brought offerings of eggs and cream and Martha Dempsey's peach preserves.

" The Babe pretty nigh lives on this side of the river now. I 'low I ought to help victual the camp."

" We can't do without him," said the girl. " He makes all our good times."

" The Babe seems to be growin' older-like this summer," mused his father. " He ain't to say manlier, but he 's different."

" Do you think so?" said Miss Brooks, startled. Her color faded to ivory. She was sitting in a hammock, and occasionally stretched out a sandaled foot to propel it. The old man felt her beauty with a dumb jealousy of all bright young creatures who had not been robbed, like his boy, of their birthright.

Jerome came later in the afternoon, and

found his daily companion still in her hammock, but changed toward him.

He had just finished an æolian harp for her. It had required days to properly season the wood, and other days to assort the colors and dry the glue which held different layers together. The instrument was a thing of beauty, with even little keys to wind the strings. He had worked over it with all his faculties excited; and now when he stood before her, holding it very tenderly on his arm, she scarcely looked at it.

But Jerome knew what to do. He moved off with his harp and fixed it in the low fork of a tree. Then he raised its bridges, and turned to watch her face. The harp sighed, and began on a high key " The Last Rose of Summer," but after two or three bars, lost its score in a flood of delicious organ harmonies. Now it rose to a cry in the zenith, and now it returned to the " Last Rose," and died to a whisper of melody. It was the passionate revelation of a human heart.

Jerome smiled and nodded his head ; for the girl's chin and lips trembled. She let her book slip down the hammock.

" Talks," insisted Jerome, claiming her attention for the harp. " I made it to talk to you."

" But it 's so sorrowful," said Lilian.

" It — isn 't — quite right," explained Jerome. " Can't carry its tune."

" And you made it for me ? "

" Yes. I been a month."

" You do too much for me. I have been very selfish to take so much of your time."

Jerome put up his lip like a grieved child.

" Don't do that ! " said Miss Brooks sharply, blanching white.

" What must I do ? "

" Sit down here, and let me read to you."

He sat on the grass and she read austerely, the weird heart-cry of the wind harp curving around her voice or whipping it with ravelings of sweetness. She read while the sun slipped lower and lower, and dared not look at the rapt face watching her. Then she shut the book and said with careful modulation: —

" Thank you very much for the wind harp. I shall take it home with me, and whenever it plays I shall think of you."

His grieved lip instantly smiled. ". If you fasten it in your window it will play all the time ! "

" There is one other thing I would love to have, and that is a feather from Billy."

Jerome stretched out an arm and drew his familiar toward him. Billy twitched his short tail and curved a suspicious neck while his master stretched one glistening pinion.

" Do you want his whole wing ? " inquired Jerome, groping for a knife.

" Not for the world ! " exclaimed Miss Brooks. " Only one of dear Billy's tiniest feathers, to put away and look at."

Jerome plucked a quill and handed it to her.

" You may have him all, if you want him."

" But what would you do without Billy ? "

He repeated, " Do without ? " several times, turning the suggestion in his mind, and gazing at her.

A couple of hours later Miss Brooks said to her brother : —

" Eric, I believe I will go home at once."

" Guess not," responded the captain. " We shift camp next week. I want you to stay until then. Are n't you having a good time ? "

" I 've been bathing too much in the river, perhaps. Mr. Marsh says it 's aguish. I shall have ague if I stay."

" The doctor is coming," said her brother.

" I must go home, Eric ; indeed, I must ! "

" You can't wait until Jack arrives, I suppose ? "

" Jack ! Is Jack coming ? "

" We were going to surprise you ; one of

the men rowed to the station for him this afternoon."

Miss Brooks's face expressed lively antici- pation.

" Jack is coming ! Then I may run back with him to-morrow, without waiting longer for Marie."

" Don't you want to give the poor fellow any taste of the camp ? " demanded her in- dignant brother.

The wind harp, rousing from silence, burst out again with the bars it would never finish, and meandered into saddening minors.

" What machine is making that doleful sound ? "

Lilian turned her tragic face away. Be- fore Jack arrived she had taken down Je- rome's offering, wrapped it carefully, and hid it in the heart of her luggage. The spirit of the Wabash gave this large and engaging young arrival its cold shoulder. Not a drop of rain had tarnished the sun- shine in a month ; but he reached camp in

a chill drizzle. The wind became so sharp
that evening fires were built. The river
hissed against its banks ; and the cook re-
ported a broken trot-line, and consequent
failure in the catch of fish.

" This is fine ! " commented Jack, turning
up his collar as he smoked with the captain,
and Lilian huddled to the fire. " Every letter has been full of the pleasures of camp
life ; and now I experience them myself ! "

" Give the camp a chance," remonstrated
Eric. " You could n't drag me back to
town ! Six months in a year, thank heaven !
I am a man ! I live outdoors, free from the
trammels of a soft civilization ! "

" We don't mind the trammels of a soft
civilization, do we, Jack ? " said the girl,
snugly slipping her hand into her lover's.

Jerome appeared at the other side of the
campfire, looking through thin smoke at
her. He had his violin bag on his shoulder.

" Hello ! " the civil engineer hailed him.
" Pull up a chunk, and sit down, Jerome."

Lilian ran to her own tent for another camp-chair. But Jerome stood still, outside the wilderness hearth, and looked at the stranger whose every imposing line was illuminated by the fire, and who acknowledged his presence with a nod.

"One of our neighbors from the Illinois side," explained the captain.

"Is n't the river rough to-night?" inquired Miss Brooks.

Jerome heard the tremor in her voice. He answered "Yes."

"It was so good of you to come. I wanted to hear you play once more. We may go home to-morrow."

"Sit down, boy," urged the captain; while Jack smoked peacefully.

"No," said Jerome. "I 'll play out there."

"Out where?"

"Out there; on the moving water."

"But I want to talk to you!" exclaimed Lilian, following him a step, relaxing under the eye of the man she was to marry. "I want to send messages to your father and aunt — I may not see them again."

" Singular chap," observed Jack as Jerome walked on into darkness.

" Half witted," explained Eric.

" He's not half witted! " vehemently denied Lilian.

" Quarter witted, then," amended her brother.

" He's an unfortunate child, lost out of paradise, at the mercy of careless, cruel wretches like us below. I never saw a woman with a nature so spotless."

" It occurs to me you're partial to your Wabash angel," observed Jack.

Jerome began to play. He was evidently in his boat plunging with the current. One could imagine him pressing against his neck the instrument which holds the saddest possibilities of sound. It wailed down river, and ceased. After an interval it began again up river. Jerome had rowed back against the current, and he went floating past the camp once more, pouring through the violin the vagaries of a mind in double darkness.

"If the trot-line was n't already broken, he 'd break it," remarked Captain Eric, "raking back and forth."

"Fine cheerful banshee for a night like this," said Jack.

Lilian huddled by the end of a log, where she could hear the oozing sap complain. Again the music died on the river, and again it began farther up, with an orchestral support of lashing water and gathering weather.

"I can't stand it!" she cried out, rising from her place. "I 'm going to my tent."

"Why did you set Jerome on?" inquired her brother in surprise. "He never knows when to quit. I 'll put a stop to it."

So going close to the shore he shouted such a peremptory request as virile man offers to weaklings. He patronized Jerome also, representing that the water was too rough for a boy, and recommending the boy to go home.

Yet hours afterwards when the campfire smouldered, and the trees were wrestling, Lilian, sobbing and smothering her face with her pillow, heard the violin once more, playing softly in imitation of the wind harp.

Next morning the river was a valley of black and sulphurous vapors, like a smoking volcanic fissure. The ague season had undoubtedly set in. Captain Eric and a squad of his men rowed their departing guests and the young lady's luggage up river to the steamboat landing, and from this the party walked to a station in the woods.

There was a bustle about tickets and checking. The station-master hurried out of his small general store with the mail-bag on his arm, for the train was already in sight.

Miss Brooks's hair clung in damp rings to her face. She turned to impress woods and water stretches upon her mind in one last glance, and her lips went white. Behind her stood Jerome, the porcelain quality of his face increased tenfold, the blueness of his eyes pierced by the keen anguish of a man. She crossed the platform to him, took his head between her hands, and rising on tiptoe kissed his forehead.

Immediately afterwards she was handed up the railway carriage steps, and Jack was making a place for her and her traveling bag. The little station slid away. She had forgotten to wave to Eric one of the hands which trembled as she adjusted her belongings over and over.

" Don't say a word to me," she commanded, meeting her lover's eyes. " I did n't know I was going to do it. I intend to marry you, Jack, because I would rather have you for a husband than any other man in the world. But he was my playmate. He brought back my childhood to me, and in return I gave him a wound ! "

Quite a year passed before she had fur-

ther news of the Babe Jerome. Her brother moved his camp two days after her
departure, and stayed out until November.
The following summer Lilian and her husband came face to face with Mr. Marsh in
that magic White City which stood a brief
season beside Lake Michigan. The blue
cape was not around his shoulders, but some
other incongruous garment marked him.
Lilian grasped his hand. He greeted the
young pair. His hairy cheeks were sunken,
and the keenness of his eye appeared dulled.

" Are Jerome and his Aunt Betsey with
you ? "

" The Babe has gone off with the quick
consumption that took his mother," said the
old man, and Lilian became aware that her
nails must be cutting his hand. She gasped,
but could not say a word.

" Yes ; Betsey and me 's alone now," he
pursued. " I brung her up to the World's
Fair to turn her mind off it. . . . He never
done well in the new house. I locked it up

and carried him back to his log cradle. But the Babe had to go. I took him to Floridy, and I took him to Colorado. . . . I had n't orto repine at affliction. He was a good Babe. . . . He made a wind harp, like, and put it in the winder, in the teeth of the air; and that was all his interest, to listen while it played."

Lilian found her husband supporting her, while water and sky and white palaces and hurrying people swam giddily in a far-off circle. She said "Thank you," and clutched his arm.

"Sis here, she liked the Babe," continued the old father, forced to wipe his eyes on the corner of a red handkerchief which he drew half way out of his side pocket. "And the Babe he liked her. I reelly thought he was pinin' sometimes for young folks; for he done well while you was there. . . . Billy — you recollect Billy the gander? He takes it to heart like a dog. . . . I'm glad I seen you. I was goin' along feelin' too bitter in my thoughts about the Babe."

Silently parting company, the old man walked on amidst wonders which he scarcely noticed, and the young pair turned aside from the crowds.

" Oh Jack ! " said Lilian, when she could control her weeping, " I have killed the Babe Jerome ! "

THE CALHOUN FIDDLER

TIME, 1890

NOVEMBER frost lay on the ferns and mosses along the Calhoun bluffs, and on that castellated mass of rock with round turrets which hangs over the cove known as French Hollow. From a divide in wooded hills a small stream came down unfrozen, quivering over pebbles and clean sand. Crossing an alluvial plat of ground, it turned beside a cabin to meet the broad and whispering Illinois.

In all Calhoun County, that long narrow ridge isolated between two great rivers, there was not on height or in cove such another cabin. It was fifty-two feet square and two stories high, with a Norman projection of the eaves. The house, with its back to a road winding at the foot of the bluffs, sat ·facing the historic Illinois — a river now yellow and wrathful with floods, now spreading in blue or seashell tints away to the opposite forest.

In the days of old Antoine Dejarnet, the builder of this log-house and the first Frenchman who ever set foot in Calhoun County, hospitality had overflowed the now silent place. Then there was dancing every Sunday after mass, in the undivided lower story like a feudal hall; and the family violin was coaxed to heavenly tunes by Antoine Dejarnet himself.

But long before this November afternoon the French colony in Calhoun County had dwindled to a remnant; the forty goats which used to climb those heights or stand captive to half old Antoine's many daughters while the rest milked them, had not a single descendant; and the last Dejarnet carried his name locally disfigured into De Zhirley.

Jeanne Sattory, following a road beside the stream, was coming down the hollow.

The mail-carrier cantered below her toward Kampsville, riding a nervous pony, and having the letter pouch strapped behind him. Twice a week he thus carried news through Calhoun County, where there are neither railroads nor telegraph lines, neither banks nor thieves. But such a courier feels his freedom and importance; he impudently kissed his merry finger-tips to the pretty girl up the slope. She hid behind a rock until he was out of sight. The mail-carrier had seen this girl before, and desired to have a closer look at her. The usual type in Calhoun County was the broad Dutch maid, whose stock had superseded the French. But Jeanne Sattory felt a dread rising to terror of all men. Her first recollection was of a stepfather who had made her take to trees like a cat, every time he approached the dwelling. Her next was of his son, who finished the small rites of her mother's funeral by taking the orphan's ear in his grip, leading her to the limit of the garden patch, and dismissing her, with the threat of a kick if she ever came back there again. He kept her mother's own household goods and the few belongings left by her father, and nobody took it in hand to interfere with him. She came back across the Illinois River to her native county, but even yet shrank from old Henry Roundcounter, whose family afforded her a home.

The Rencontres had held land under the first Dejarnet. As Roundcounters, and farmers of their own small holding, they now kept up hereditary interest in that last De Zhirley who, since his mother's death, had lived solitary in the great square cabin. Mrs. Roundcounter baked bread for him; and once a week she went down the bluff to tidy his bachelor hall, except when rheumatism detained her. This afternoon Jeanne Sattory was sent reluctantly to the task.

The last De Zhirley was a ferryman; and it must be owned that voices calling him from the other side of the river were often drowned in the music of his fiddle. In clear summer nights he walked a sandy strip in front of his cabin, hugging the fiddle beneath his chin and playing tunes which had come down from his forefathers.

The ferryboat could now be seen at the farther bank of the Illinois. Jeanne knew she might do her work before it could again cross the current. The cabin door is always left unfastened in that primitive county. She noticed a fresh coon skin nailed on the logs beside the door, as with shrinking she entered this haunt of man.

The imposing old dancing-hall of the De Zhirleys gave her a welcome from its ruddy fireplace hooded with a penthouse. Jeanne's first care was to push the embers together, heap on more of the wood which lay ready, and clean the stone hearth. She then hung a pot on the crane, and filled it with spring water. Before the water was scalding hot there was time to sweep the floor and beat up a feather bed which had grown as hard as a mat on its corner bedstead.

An unrailed stairway mounted beside the front wall. Jeanne had heard Mrs. Round-counter tell how many little rooms were overhead, and what stores of family goods were piled there, disregarded by a young man who cared for no wife but his fiddle.

No attention could be given to the upper rooms. Amid all her services, the girl was full of starts and panics, turning her head and widening her eyes at any stir without. She mopped the broad boards worn by foot-marks of dead dancers; she washed log imbedded windows and an accumulation of yellow bowls and pewter; and drew the only easy chair to the hearth. Something in a green bag hung on the wall farthest from the fire, which Jeanne knew to be the De Zhirley fiddle. She touched it carefully with a turkey-wing duster, recoiling from its faint ting as if some charm had been ignorantly worked.

Dried meat and scarlet peppers, a gun and powderhorn hung on the richly smoked hewn joists. She felt keen, quiet delight in the place, and reluctance to leave it. The jollity of former times, perhaps, lingered, making a fit atmosphere for girlhood.

But she was standing with her shawl over her head, casting back a last look, when some hand blundered at the latch outside. She sprang upstairs and put the first door between her and the intruder on the lightning of impulse. Some person entered and seemed to pause and listen suspiciously. Her heart labored like the beating of a steamer, and she expected to hear feet following her up the stairs. But after uncertain shuffling the comer dragged a chair, and, with a suggestion of effort, sat down.

Jeanne knew it could not be young De Zhirley, whom she had just seen through a window fighting the current in midriver. He had a loaded wagon and a pair of restless mules on board ; and he ran back and forth outside the railing of his boat, now poling, now steering, and now pulling with a wing-

like oar. Jeanne could have been at the top
of the bluff before his return. And here she
was, trapped in an upper room, vaguely
ashamed; unable to come down and face
eyes which might insult her, yet terrified by
the prospect of indefinite hiding.

Daylight's gradual fading out was of more
interest to her than the accumulation of De
Zhirley things around her. She listened for
the crunch of the ferryboat prow on gravel;
and voices and departing wheels at last
moved by the cabin, and the proper owner
entered. She stealthily unlatched her door
and set it ajar, so the crack intersected the
hearth. There in the seat she had taken
thought to set ready sagged the drunken
person of her stepbrother.

" You here, Billy Aarons?" said young De
Zhirley, as he approached the fire; and his
voice had no joy in it. His blind eye was
toward the stair door, for the Calhoun fiddler was a one-eyed man. This defacement
scarcely marred the beauty of the athletic

man thrown out by firelight. Jeanne Sattory had, indeed, never seen him without pitying people who were two-eyed. His misused skin yet held the milk and wine flush of childhood, and his fleece of red-gold rings was a gift not to be spoiled.

" Yes, I 'm here, Theodore," said the man in the chair thickly.

" Mother Roundcounter has been here too," added De Zhirley, as he looked about. " It makes a feller feel good to see his house clean and smell new bread."

ᐟ He hung a teakettle on the crane, and thrust a fork through some bacon to toast on the polished hearthstone. Then he drew his table toward the fireplace, and Jeanne could see his appreciative touch on the yellow ware she had washed.

" What do you want, Billy? Did you come in to take a bite with me ? "

" No." Aarons stirred from his doze. " I 'm buyin' cattle, Theodore."

" No cattle to sell here."

"I know it, Theodore. You're a poor man by the side of me."

Indifferent to this fact, De Zhirley turned his bacon and proceeded to make coffee.

"You're a poor man, Theodore," repeated the heavy guest, "and I've got all my father had."

"And all his second wife had," added young De Zhirley, with a one-eyed glance of contempt, at which Aarons made a fist. "You go upstairs and sleep off what's the matter with you, after I give you some coffee."

"That's not what I come for. You're a poor man, Theodore."

"Well, don't let that keep you awake; it don't me."

"You hain't got no cattle, nor much land, nor even two eyes."

"And what do *you* want on my blind side, Billy?"

"But you've got a fiddle. Yes; you've got a fiddle."

De Zhirley moved back and took his violin off the wall with a jealous motion. It was his custom to play while his supper cooked; but as he felt the bow with his thumb, and fitted the instrument to his neck, he looked distrustfully at Aarons.

The first sweet long cry filled the cabin. The fiddler gradually approached the hearth, playing as he came, and Aarons's head, hands, and feet responded to the magic.

De Zhirley's back was toward Jeanne, but she saw joy in his whole bearing, and herself felt the piercing rapture of sound.

" Let me see that fiddle," demanded Aarons, when the young man finished and put down his bow, and brought the coffee-pot to set on the coals.

De Zhirley turned a distrustful eye, but no precious violin toward his guest.

" Let me see that fiddle, I say," repeated Aarons, rising up.

" Behave yourself," said the young man, standing a head above him, and humoring him as a child might be humored by half granting his request.

The fellow handled its ancient body, and looked at Stradivari's inscription.

"What's that there, Theodore?"

"That's the maker's name."

"Seventeen hunderd and — what's them figgers?"

"That's the year it was made."

"Then it's a mighty poor old thing, ain't it?"

The fiddler said nothing, but tried to recover his violin, to which the tormentor hung with both hands.

"I can sell it for you, Theodore. It's worth fifty dollars."

De Zhirley's face expressed impatience to regain his instrument.

"Yes, it's worth a hunderd dollars. I've been talkin' with a man, Theodore; that's why I come in. You give this fiddle to me, and I'll make some money for you. You're a poor man, Theodore."

"Let go of it," exclaimed De Zhirley. "I don't want to sell my fiddle."

"It's worth five hunderd dollars."

"Let go of it! You don't know what you're doing. You ain't fit to do anything now. Let go," cried De Zhirley, as he felt the greedy, drunken hands crushing his treasure. "If you don't let go, I'll kill you!"

The two men struggled, and there was a crackling, twanging sound, followed by Aarons's curses. Then De Zhirley caught him by the neck, dragged him to the cabin door, and kicked him far out into the dusk.

Jeanne hid her face. She heard her stepbrother battering at the fastened door, and finally a stone dashed through the window, to fall with splintered glass upon the floor. A storm of drunken curses surrounded the house and died away in mutterings along the bluff road. Through this clamor an awful silence made its void in the cabin.

De Zhirley had set his foot upon a chair, and was nursing the mangled instrument on his knee, examining every part. His tense face denied despair; but the broken neck hung down by its strings, the chest was crushed, the back split, the bridge lay beside his foot. Jeanne watched him, forgetting the darkness of the bluffs and her dreadful ambush.

When De Zhirley first came in she had decided to let herself down from an upper window rather than face him. When he recommended her stepbrother to a sleeping-room upstairs, she looked about in panic for something which could be made an immediate rope or ladder. But when she saw the violin's destruction, it was to hang outside that tragedy in a passion of sympathy. She had been the most solitary creature in Calhoun County, but this supreme sharing of the young fiddler's anguish broke the shell of her dumbness; she felt her soul spreading out its crumpled wings like a new butterfly.

He laid the violin on the chair, and with a sudden abandonment of all restraint shook

his fists above his head, wailing and sobbing : —

" Oh, my Lord, my Lord! What will I do
now?"

It was the agony of an artist, of a lonely
soul, of unspeakable bereavement.

Jeanne wept in her shawl. She had thought
her hunger for the unknown best thing in
the world a singular experience. She waited
until his tears and hers could be wiped off,
and then opened the door and came lightly
downstairs.

De Zhirley huddled his violin again in his
arms, as if dreading the descent of more
drunken men, and, in the embarrassment
and anguish of a man whose weakness has
been spied upon, turned his face to the
hearth. Jeanne stopped at the foot of the
stairs and drew her shawl over her head.
They continued in silence while the coffee
bubbled up and firelight flickered on the
wall.

De Zhirley understood her errand into his

cabin with the simplicity of primitive man-
hood. He knew she always took to flight
when her stepbrother appeared. When he
could speak without a sob, he said, acknow-
ledging all she had done for his comfort that
afternoon : —

" I 'm much obleeged."

Jeanne, on her part, ignored the services.

" Is it bad hurt?" she murmured, with
unconscious maternal pathos.

He offered to yield the wreck to her
hands, and, drawn from her place, she went
and stooped on one knee to the firelight. De
Zhirley dropped on one knee beside her, and
they tried to fit the mangled parts in place
again.   •

" It 's such a spite," said Jeanne, and her
trembling voice comforted him as a mother
comforts her child. He had instant anxiety
to make the calamity appear less to her than
it really was.

" Mebby by patchin' and glue I can put
it together again — though I don't know

whether it'll sound the same. I've always thought so much of it," he apologized.

"I wish he had broke my neck instead of this fiddle's," said the girl with passion.

"I'd like to see him try such a thing as that," responded the fiddler sternly. "I'd killed him as't was, if I hadn't been bigger than him."

"I must go back," exclaimed Jeanne, stirring to rise from this post-mortem. "They'll think I've fell in the river."

"I'll go with you," said De Zhirley. "It's dark now, and that fellow ain't gone far."

"No," objected Jeanne, with sudden terror of what her neighborhood called a beau. "I don't want no one with me."

De Zhirley took up his cap with gentle insistence like the courtliness of a great seignior. He smiled at Jeanne, and she gave him back a look of which she was unconscious.

"Your supper's all ready," she reminded him.

"I ain't hungry like I was when I come in from the ferry. Won't you set down and take supper with me?" invited the young man sincerely.

The mere suggestion sent Jeanne Sattory to the door. Their hands mingled upon the latch, and she slid hers away, loath to part from a touch which she yet eluded.

De Zhirley made the door pause while he looked down at her and said, with a shaking voice: —

"If it had n't been for you — there ain't no tellin'."

Jeanne had no reply to this acknowledgment of sympathy, but drew her shawl together under her chin. Chin and mouth-corners were tempting even to a one-eyed man, but he continued with gentle courtesy:

"Spite of my fiddle's gettin' broke, I b'lieve this is the best day this cabin ever seen."

"What makes you say that?"

"'Cause it 's the first time you ever come to the house."

" I 'm obleeged for your politeness," trembled Jeanne, turning scarlet; and she lifted a laughing dark glance. " If you 'll be a little politer and let me out, I won't come no more."

" Then I 'll go where you are," declared the Calhoun fiddler. " I 'll foller you from this time on."

" You 'll have to walk on the other side of the road if you do," said Jeanne Sattory ; and they stepped out and took the way up the bluff, two figures indistinct in darkness, with a width of wagon-track between them.

A MAN FROM THE SPANISH WAR

*A conversation in Egypt, which is an undefined
region of Southern Illinois*

TIME, 1898

MISS LUCY MILLS waited with three
early arrivals in her sitting-room. The rest
of the people would not gather for half an
hour. Her wide house, venerable for the
region in which it stood, hugged by vines
and mossy roofed, was in perfect order ; and
sheaves of flowers exhaled fragrance around
an object placed in the centre of her parlor.
Neighbors no longer trod about on tiptoe,
for everything was ready, and the minister
might arrive at any moment.

Miss Lucy sat a dignified spinster, whose
sympathies ramified through the entire human race. She was so homely that strangers
turned to look at her as at a beauty. Mr.

Sammy Blade was in his thirties, but she considered him a youth, having helped his mother to nurse him through measles and whooping-cough. Mr. Sammy had a protruding pointed beard and rolled his silly bald head on his shoulders when he talked. He had studied medicine but, failing of practice, was turning his attention to the peddling of fruit-trees. Coming home and hearing the news, he hastened to appear at Miss Lucy's house.

Mr. and Mrs. Plankson had returned to the neighborhood to visit. The husband was a frisky gray little man, and his wife was a jimp woman in stiff black silk with large lips and shifty eyes.

All three of Miss Lucy's callers coughed and made the unconscious grimaces of plain people who have not learned the art of expression. They sat with their hands piled on their stomachs. Yet while they longed to get at facts which only Miss Lucy knew, they approached these facts roundabout, bringing newsy bits of their own, and avoiding by common instinct the subject of war with Spain.

" Have you heard that Emeline Smith's oldest girl has experienced religion ? " inquired Mr. Sammy solemnly, breaking the silence of the down-sitting after greetings.

" No, I had n't heard it," responded Miss Lucy, in the soft slow drawl which her candid speech made its vehicle.

" Law me ! " exclaimed Mrs. Plankson, " Emeline Smith was always a great hand for revivals. If she had went less to meetings and had saw more to do in her own house, her children would be better brung up."

" Seem-me-like there is some spite-work against Emeline Smith amongst the women," observed Mr. Plankson. " I was a beau of Emeline's onct. I went to see her the other day, and she laughed, and waved the broom, and acted so glad Jane can't get over it."

" You orto married her," said Mrs. Plankson crisply. " You 'd be richer than you
are. Her mother was the savin'est person
I ever heard of. She give a tea-party one
time, and the milk floated in lumps on top
the cups. She said she did n't see how it
could be sour, when she had put saleratus in
it and boiled it twice ! Them Smiths got
their money from a rich old aunt, that used
to cut up squares of tissue paper to make
handkerchiefs. I seen her one time myself,
when she was a-visiting the Smiths, come to
meeting with a wreath of live geranium
leaves around her bonnet, in winter, and
them leaves all bit black with the cold!
We 've heard she would set before the parlor
fire in city hotels where she boarded, with
her dress turned up on her knees, showing
her little sticks of legs in narrow pantalets
and white stockings, just to save fire in her
room — and young ladies obliged to receive
young men, with her a-setting there ! "

Mr. Sammy coughed gently, for Mrs.

Plankson had overlooked his presence in her wrath against Emeline Smith's relations.

To cover the situation her husband directly inquired, " What 's become of them Ellison girls, seven sisters, that all dressed alike and carried umberellas the same color ? They used to walk into church in Indian file.   I never in my life seen them go two or three abreast."

" They all live where they used to and look like they always did.   For they was born old-like.   Carline," said Miss Lucy, " took to herb doctorin'.   Along about the time that President Garfield was shot, Carline got very dissatisfied.   ' I know just what would fetch that bullet out,' she used to say, ' and the only thing that would fetch it out.' "

" And what was that ? " inquired Mr. Sammy, rounding his lips and stretching his short neck forward.

" Spearmint tea ! "

Mrs. Plankson beat her right palm softly

on her left forearm and leaned over, shaking. It would not have been decorous to cackle out loud. The American flag and its Cuban little sister, draped together around the wide doorway of the parlor, swayed in the air. She glanced through the open portal, her oblique eyes slanting up to Miss Lucy's hanging lamp decorated with feathery asparagus.

" Carline told my niece," Mrs. Plankson added to the Ellison subject, " why she never got married."

" " Did she have a disappointment? " inquired Mr. Sammy, as one of the younger generation, who fully sensed a woman's loss in not obtaining a companion like himself.

" No. ' Do you know,' says she to my niece, ' why I never got married?' ' No,' says my niece, ' I don't.' — ' Tew skittish !' says Carline."

" I never seen such a neighborhood as this is for old maids !" exclaimed Mr. Plankson.

Miss Lucy regarded him with a virgin's

pitying tolerance. Homely as she was, she thought it would have been impossible for her to have taken up with the likes of William Plankson in his best days.

" There has been too much marryin' and givin' in marriage in this neighborhood," she declared with her soft drawl.

" Seem-me-like you ain't no good judge of that, Lucy," bantered Mr. Plankson.

" It 's Emeline Smith that 's the judge," thrust in his wife.

Miss Lucy contemplated silently.

" I was thinkin' of Jaw-awn and Sue Emma," she said ; and the other three composed themselves to hear the facts concerning the man from the Spanish war. With a rustle like that of a congregation settling to the sermon after preliminaries, they moved their feet and hands and waited on Miss Lucy.

" I was against the match, for Sue Emma had been married, and was through with it. Her man died and left her with a farm and two children ; and a widow well fixed is a sight better off than a married woman."

Mrs. Plankson gave involuntary assent and then glanced with oblique apprehension at her husband, whose will was made in her favor.

" But Sue Emma was n't of Yankee stock like the Ellison girls. She felt pestered to get along by herself."

" Seem-me-like a man always is needed on a farm," put in Mr. Plankson.

" Sue Emma thought that-a-way. But I talked reel plain to her when she took up with Jaw-awn. I had n't nothing against Jaw-awn, except he was a man. He was without property, but he was mighty good to Sue Emma and the children. Seem-like he thought as much of the children as he did of her. And when they had been married a couple of years and the new baby come, Jaw-awn would have been tickled to death if it had n't been for losin' it and Sue Emma. Now that woman might have been livin' to-day if she had let men alone. But Jaw-awn was a great hand for his folks. I thought he would go crazy. Seem-like he could neither lay nor set when he come home from buryin' Sue Emma and the baby; but just wandered around, Lolly Loo and the little boy holdin' one onto each of his hands."

"Lolly Loo?" challenged Mrs. Plank-son. "What-for name is that?"

"Laura Louise; but they called her Lolly Loo. Jaw-awn nacherly had to have folks to do for. I believe he would have got along reel well with the children, if he had been let alone; for he was a good manager.

"But Sue Emma's father and mother moved right onto the place after the funeral, and the first thing they done was to turn Jaw-awn out. I suppose he had rights in law, but he did n't make no stand for rights; what he seemed to want was folks. He'd been an orphan-like, without father or mother, and knocked around the world and got kind of homesick clean through. Gettin' Sue Emma and her children was the same to him as comin' into a fortune, and when he was throwed out of them he give up.

" The children, they felt terrible, for they thought so much of Jaw-awn; and cried and begged.

" ' Jaw-awn won't be no trouble, gram-maw,' says Lolly Loo. ' I can cook enough for Jaw-awn to eat, if you let him stay.'

" But the old couple, they up and throwed him out. And when he stopped here on his way to Springfield I could see the man was clean broke down.

" The very next thing, along come this excitement about war with Spain, and I seen Jaw-awn's name among the volunteers. I knowed he wouldn't ever get through the war. Sure enough, word come —. I tele-graphed to have him sent here. I knowed the children's grandpaw and grandmaw wouldn't do it. And I sent them word, but they don't want to excite the children, so none of that family will come.

" I don't say nothing about the expense :
I have some means. But when I think of
them children that he was a father to — him
being so wrapped up in his folks — and
them slippin' to the bars like they do to see
if Jaw-awn is comin' back and not even
knowin' that he lays a soldier in his coffin
in that parlor — without any folks to drop
a tear on him — I feel like as if things was
wrong ! "

Miss Lucy arose and entered the parlor.
She rearranged the American and Cuban
flags which draped the plain casket, and
touched the flowers and a huge wreath bearing the initials G. A. R.

Her three guests followed her in silent
awe. She had wiped her eyes and was
ready to add, —

" The minister has took for his text, ' He
setteth the solitary in families.' I hope
everybody will turn out. The weather is
nice. Some will come because he is the
first soldier buried here from the Spanish

war, and the Grand Army Post has took it up and will march and fire a salute over his grave. I don't know as the dead care anything about it, but I'd kind of like to see Jaw-awn have as nice a funeral as if he had folks."

ELECTROTYPED AND PRINTED
BY H. O. HOUGHTON AND CO.

The Riverside Press

CAMBRIDGE, MASS., U. S. A.